Life's Secret
&
Other Folk-Tales

Life's Secret

&

Other Folk-Tales

Lal Behari Dey

Illustrations by
Warwick Goble

HAWK PRESS

Published by

Hawk Press
4836/24, Ansari Road, Daryaganj
New Delhi – 110 002
Phones : 9643330713, +91-11-23278618, +91-11-35676207
E-mail: thehawkpress@gmail.com
www.thehawkpress.com

Contents

TO
RICHARD CARNAC TEMPLE
CAPTAIN, BENGAL STAFF CORPS
F.R.G.S., M.R.A.S., M.A.I., ETC.
WHO FIRST SUGGESTED TO THE WRITER
THE IDEA OF COLLECTING
THESE TALES
AND WHO IS DOING SO MUCH
IN THE CAUSE OF INDIAN FOLK-LORE
THIS LITTLE BOOK
IS INSCRIBED

Preface

In my *Peasant Life in Bengal* I make the peasant boy Govinda spend some hours every evening in listening to stories told by an old woman, who was called Sambhu's mother, and who was the best story-teller in the village. On reading that passage, Captain R. C. Temple, of the Bengal Staff Corps, son of the distinguished Indian administrator Sir Richard Temple, wrote to me to say how interesting it would be to get a collection of those unwritten stories which old women in India recite to little children in the evenings, and to ask whether I could not make such a collection. As I was no stranger to the *Mährchen* of the Brothers Grimm, to the Norse Tales so admirably told by Dasent, to Arnason's *Icelandic Stories* translated by Powell, to the *Highland Stories* done into English by Campbell, and to the fairy stories collected by other writers, and as I believed that the collection suggested would be a contribution, however slight, to that daily increasing literature of folk-lore and comparative mythology which, like comparative philosophy, proves that the swarthy and half-naked peasant on the banks of the Ganges is a cousin, albeit of the hundredth remove, to the fair-skinned and well-dressed Englishman on the banks of the Thames, I readily caught up the idea and cast about for materials. But where was an old story-telling woman to be got? I had myself, when a little boy, heard hundreds—it would be no exaggeration to say thousands—of fairy tales from that same old woman, Sambhu's mother—for she was no fictitious person; she actually lived in the flesh and bore that name; but I had nearly forgotten those stories, at any rate they had all got confused in my head, the tail of one story being joined to the head of another, and the head of a third to the tail of a fourth.

How I wished that poor Sambhu's mother had been alive! But she had gone long, long ago, to that bourne from which no traveller returns, and her son Sambhu, too, had followed her thither. After a great deal of search I found my Gammer Grethel—though not half so old as the Frau Viehmännin of Hesse-Cassel—in the person of a Bengali Christian woman, who, when a little girl and living in her heathen home, had heard many stories from her old grandmother. She was a good story-teller, but her stock was not large; and after I had heard ten from her I had to look about for fresh sources. An old Brahman told me two stories; an old barber, three; an old servant of mine told me two; and the rest I heard from another old Brahman. None of my authorities knew English; they all told the stories in Bengali, and I translated them into English when I came home. I heard many more stories than those contained in the following pages; but I rejected a great many, as they appeared to me to contain spurious additions to the original stories which I had heard when a boy. I have reason to believe that the stories given in this book are a genuine sample of the old old stories told by old Bengali women from age to age through a hundred generations.

Sambhu's mother used always to end every one of her stories—and every orthodox Bengali story-teller does the same—with repeating the following formula:—

Thus my story endeth,
The Natiya-thorn withereth.
"Why, O Natiya-thorn, dost wither?"
"Why does thy cow on me browse?"
"Why, O cow, dost thou browse?"
"Why does thy neat-herd not tend me?"
"Why, O neat-herd, dost not tend the cow?"
"Why does thy daughter-in-law not give me rice?"
"Why, O daughter-in-law, dost not give rice?"
"Why does my child cry?"
"Why, O child, dost thou cry?"
"Why does the ant bite me?"
"Why, O ant, dost thou bite?"
Koot! koot! koot!

What these lines mean, why they are repeated at the end of every story, and what the connection is of the several parts to one another, I do not know. Perhaps the whole is a string of nonsense purposely put together to amuse little children.

Lal Behari Day
Hooghly College,
February 27, 1883.

1

Life's Secret

There was a king who had two queens, Duo and Suo.[1] Both of them were childless. One day a Faquir (mendicant) came to the palace-gate to ask for alms. The Suo queen went to the door with a handful of rice. The mendicant asked whether she had any children. On being answered in the negative, the holy mendicant refused to take alms, as the hands of a woman unblessed with child are regarded as ceremonially unclean. He offered her a drug for removing her barrenness, and she expressing her willingness to receive it, he gave it to her with the following directions:—"Take this nostrum, swallow it with the juice of the pomegranate flower; if you do this, you will have a son in due time. The son will be exceedingly handsome, and his complexion will be of the colour of the pomegranate flower; and you shall call him Dalim Kumar.[2] As enemies will try to take away the life of your son, I may as well tell you that the life of the boy will be bound up in the life of a big boal fish which is in your tank, in front of the palace. In the heart of the fish is a small box of wood, in the box is a necklace of gold, that necklace is the life of your son. Farewell."

"The Suo queen went to the door with a handful of rice"

In the course of a month or so it was whispered in the palace that the Suo queen had hopes of an heir. Great was the joy of the king. Visions of an heir to the throne, and of a never-ending succession of powerful monarchs perpetuating his dynasty to the latest generations, floated before his mind, and made him glad as he had never been in his life. The usual ceremonies performed on such occasions were celebrated with great pomp; and the subjects made loud demonstrations of their joy at the anticipation of so auspicious an event as the birth of a prince. In the fulness of time the Suo queen gave birth to a son of uncommon beauty. When the king the first time saw the face of the infant, his heart leaped with joy. The ceremony of the child's first rice was celebrated with extraordinary pomp, and the whole kingdom was filled with gladness.

In course of time Dalim Kumar grew up a fine boy. Of all sports he was most addicted to playing with pigeons. This brought him into frequent contact with his stepmother, the Duo queen, into whose apartments Dalim's pigeons had a trick of always flying. The first time the pigeons flew into her rooms, she readily gave them up to the owner; but the second time she gave them up with some reluctance. The fact is that the Duo queen, perceiving that Dalim's pigeons had this happy knack of flying into her apartments, wished to take advantage of it for the furtherance of her own selfish views. She naturally hated the child, as the king, since his birth, neglected her more than ever, and idolised the fortunate mother of Dalim. She had heard, it is not known how, that the holy mendicant that had given the famous pill to the Suo queen had also told her of a secret connected with the child's life. She had heard that the child's life was bound up with something—she did not know with what. She determined to extort that secret from the boy. Accordingly, the next time the pigeons flew into her rooms, she refused to give them up, addressing the child thus:—"I won't give the pigeons up unless you tell me one thing."

Dalim. What thing, mamma?

Duo. Nothing particular, my darling; I only want to know in what your life is.

Dalim. What is that, mamma? Where can my life be except in me?

Duo. No, child; that is not what I mean. A holy mendicant told your mother that your life is bound up with something. I wish to know what that thing is.

Dalim. I never heard of any such thing, mamma.

Duo. If you promise to inquire of your mother in what thing your life is, and if you tell me what your mother says, then I will let you have the pigeons, otherwise not.

Dalim. Very well, I'll inquire, and let you know. Now, please, give me my pigeons.

Duo. I'll give them on one condition more. Promise to me that you will not tell your mother that I want the information.

Dalim. I promise.

The Duo queen let go the pigeons, and Dalim, overjoyed to find again his beloved birds, forgot every syllable of the conversation he had had with his stepmother. The next day, however, the pigeons again flew into the Duo queen's rooms. Dalim went to his stepmother, who asked him for the required information. The boy promised to ask his mother that very day, and begged hard for the release of the pigeons. The pigeons were at last delivered. After play, Dalim went to his mother and said— "Mamma, please tell me in what my life is contained." "What do you mean, child?" asked the mother, astonished beyond measure at the child's extraordinary question. "Yes, mamma," rejoined the child, "I have heard that a holy mendicant told you that my life is contained in something. Tell me what that thing is." "My pet, my darling, my treasure, my golden moon, do not ask such an inauspicious question. Let the mouth of my enemies be covered with ashes, and let my Dalim live for ever," said the mother, earnestly. But the child insisted on being informed of the secret. He said he would not eat or drink anything unless the information were given him. The Suo queen, pressed by the importunity of her son, in an evil hour told the child the secret of his life. The next day the pigeons again, as fate would have it, flew into the Duo queen's rooms. Dalim went for them; the stepmother plied the boy with sugared words, and obtained the knowledge of the secret.

The Duo queen, on learning the secret of Dalim Kumar's life, lost no time in using it for the prosecution of her malicious design. She told her maid-servants to get for her some dried stalks of the hemp plant, which are very brittle, and which, when pressed upon, make a peculiar noise, not unlike the cracking of joints of bones in the human body. These hemp stalks she put under her bed, upon which she laid herself down and gave out that she was dangerously ill. The king, though he did not love her so well as his other queen, was in duty bound to visit her in her illness. The queen pretended that her bones were all cracking; and sure enough, when she tossed from one side of her bed to the other, the hemp stalks made the noise wanted. The king, believing that the Duo queen was seriously ill, ordered his best physician to attend her. With that physician the Duo queen was in collusion. The physician said to the king that for the queen's complaint there was but one remedy, which consisted in the outward application of something to be found inside a large *boal* fish which was in the tank before the palace. The king's fisherman was accordingly called and ordered to catch the *boal* in question. On the first throw of the net the fish was caught. It so happened that Dalim Kumar, along with other boys, was playing not far from the tank. The moment the *boal* fish was caught in the net, that moment Dalim felt unwell; and when the fish was brought up to land, Dalim fell down on the ground, and made as if he was about to breathe his last. He was immediately taken into his mother's room, and the king was astonished on hearing of the sudden illness of his son and heir. The fish was by the order of the physician taken into the room of the Duo queen, and as it lay on the floor striking its fins on the ground, Dalim in his mother's room was given up for lost. When the fish was cut open, a casket was found in it; and in the casket lay a necklace of gold. The moment the necklace was worn by the queen, that very moment Dalim died in his mother's room.

When the news of the death of his son and heir reached the king he was plunged into an ocean of grief, which was not lessened in any degree by the intelligence of the recovery of the Duo queen. He wept over his dead Dalim so bitterly that his courtiers were apprehensive of a permanent derangement of his mental powers. The king would not allow the dead body of his son to be either buried or burnt. He could not realise the fact of his son's death; it was so entirely causeless and so terribly sudden. He ordered the dead body to be removed to one of his garden-houses in the suburbs of the city, and to be laid there in state. He ordered that all sorts of provisions should be stowed away in that house, as if the young prince needed them for his refection. Orders were issued that the house should be kept locked up day and night, and that no one should go into it except Dalim's most intimate friend, the son of the king's prime minister, who was intrusted with the key of the house, and who obtained the privilege of entering it once in twenty-four hours.

As, owing to her great loss, the Suo queen lived in retirement, the king gave up his nights entirely to the Duo queen. The latter, in order to allay suspicion, used to put aside the gold necklace at night; and, as fate had ordained that Dalim should be in the state of death only during the time that the necklace was round the neck of the queen, he passed into the state of life whenever the necklace was laid aside. Accordingly Dalim revived every night, as the Duo queen every night put away the necklace, and died again the next morning when the queen put it on. When Dalim became reanimated at night he ate whatever food he liked, for of such there was a plentiful stock in the garden-house, walked about on the premises, and meditated on the singularity of his lot. Dalim's friend, who visited him only during the day, found him always lying a lifeless corpse; but what struck him after some days was the singular fact that the body remained in the same state in which he saw it on the first day of his visit. There was no sign of putrefaction. Except that it was lifeless and pale, there were no symptoms of corruption—it was apparently quite fresh. Unable to account for so strange a phenomenon, he determined to watch the corpse more closely, and to visit it not only during the day but sometimes also at night. The first night that he paid his visit he was astounded to see his dead friend sauntering about in the garden. At first he thought the figure might be only the ghost of his friend, but on feeling him and otherwise examining him, he found the apparition to be veritable flesh and blood. Dalim related to his friend all the circumstances connected with his death; and they both concluded that he revived at nights only because the Duo queen put aside her necklace when the king visited her. As the life of the prince depended on the necklace, the two friends laid their heads together to devise if possible some plans by which they might get possession of it. Night after night they consulted together, but they could not think of any feasible scheme. At length the gods brought about the deliverance of Dalim Kumar in a wonderful manner.

Some years before the time of which we are speaking, the sister of Bidhata-Purusha[3] was delivered of a daughter. The anxious mother asked her brother what he had written on her child's forehead; to which Bidhata-Purusha replied that she should get married to a dead bridegroom. Maddened as she became with grief at the prospect of such a dreary destiny for her daughter, she yet thought it useless to remonstrate with her brother, for she well knew that he never changed what he once wrote. As the child grew in years she became exceedingly beautiful, but the mother could not look upon her with pleasure in consequence of the portion allotted to her by her divine brother. When the girl came to marriageable age, the mother resolved to flee from the country with her, and thus avert her dreadful destiny. But the decrees of fate cannot thus be overruled. In the course of their wanderings the mother and daughter arrived at the gate of that very garden-house in which Dalim Kumar lay. It was evening. The girl said she was thirsty and wanted to drink water. The mother told her daughter to sit at the gate, while she went to search for drinking water in some neighbouring hut. In the meantime the girl through curiosity pushed the door of the garden-house, which opened of itself. She then went in and saw a beautiful palace, and was wishing to come out when the door shut itself of its own accord, so that she could not get out. As night came on the prince revived, and, walking about, saw a human figure near the gate. He went up to it, and found it was a girl of surpassing beauty. On being asked who she was, she told Dalim Kumar all the details of her little history,—how her uncle, the divine Bidhata-Purusha, wrote on her forehead at her birth that she should get married to a dead bridegroom, how her mother had no pleasure in her life at the prospect of so terrible a destiny, and how, therefore, on the approach of her womanhood, with a view to avert so dreadful a catastrophe, she had left her house with her and wandered in various places, how they came to the gate of the garden-house, and how her mother had now gone in search of drinking water for her.

"The prince revived, and, walking about, saw a human figure near the gate"

Dalim Kumar, hearing her simple and pathetic story, said, "I am the dead bridegroom, and you must get married to me, come with me to the house." "How can you be said to be a dead bridegroom when you are standing and speaking to me?" said the girl. "You will understand it afterwards," rejoined the prince, "come now and follow me." The girl followed the prince into the house. As she had been fasting the whole day the prince hospitably entertained her. As for the mother of the

girl, the sister of the divine Bidhata-Purusha, she returned to
the gate of the garden-house after it was dark, cried out for her
daughter, and getting no answer, went away in search of her in
the huts in the neighbourhood. It is said that after this she was
not seen anywhere.

While the niece of the divine Bidhata-Purusha was partaking
of the hospitality of Dalim Kumar, his friend as usual made
his appearance. He was surprised not a little at the sight of
the fair stranger; and his surprise became greater when he
heard the story of the young lady from her own lips. It was
forthwith resolved that very night to unite the young couple in
the bonds of matrimony. As priests were out of the question,
the hymeneal rites were performed à la Gandharva.[4] The friend
of the bridegroom took leave of the newly-married couple and
went away to his house. As the happy pair had spent the greater
part of the night in wakefulness, it was long after sunrise that
they awoke from their sleep;—I should have said that the
young wife woke from her sleep, for the prince had become a
cold corpse, life having departed from him. The feelings of the
young wife may be easily imagined. She shook her husband,
imprinted warm kisses on his cold lips, but in vain. He was
as lifeless as a marble statue. Stricken with horror, she smote
her breast, struck her forehead with the palms of her hands,
tore her hair and went about in the house and in the garden
as if she had gone mad. Dalim's friend did not come into the
house during the day, as he deemed it improper to pay a visit
to her while her husband was lying dead. The day seemed to
the poor girl as long as a year, but the longest day has its end,
and when the shades of evening were descending upon the
landscape, her dead husband was awakened into consciousness;
he rose up from his bed, embraced his disconsolate wife, ate,
drank, and became merry. His friend made his appearance as

usual, and the whole night was spent in gaiety and festivity. Amid this alternation of life and death did the prince and his lady spend some seven or eight years, during which time the princess presented her husband with two lovely boys who were the exact image of their father.

It is superfluous to remark that the king, the two queens, and other members of the royal household did not know that Dalim Kumar was living, at any rate, was living at night. They all thought that he was long ago dead and his corpse burnt. But the heart of Dalim's wife was yearning after her mother-in-law, whom she had never seen. She conceived a plan by which she might be able not only to have a sight of her mother-in-law, but also to get hold of the Duo queen's necklace, on which her husband's life was dependent. With the consent of her husband and of his friend she disguised herself as a female barber. Like every female barber she took a bundle containing the following articles:—an iron instrument for paring nails, another iron instrument for scraping off the superfluous flesh of the soles of the feet, a piece of *jhama* or burnt brick for rubbing the soles of the feet with, and *alakta*[5] for painting the edges of the feet and toes with. Taking this bundle in her hand she stood at the gate of the king's palace with her two boys. She declared herself to be a barber, and expressed a desire to see the Suo queen, who readily gave her an interview. The queen was quite taken up with the two little boys, who, she declared, strongly reminded her of her darling Dalim Kumar. Tears fell profusely from her eyes at the recollection of her lost treasure; but she of course had not the remotest idea that the two little boys were the sons of her own dear Dalim. She told the supposed barber that she did not require her services, as, since the death of her son, she had given up all terrestrial vanities, and among others the practice of dyeing her feet red; but she added that, nevertheless, she would be glad now and then to see her and her two fine boys. The female barber, for so we must now call her, then went to the quarters of the Duo queen and offered her services. The queen allowed her to pare her nails, to scrape off the superfluous flesh of her feet, and to paint them with *alakta* and was so pleased with her skill, and the sweetness of her disposition, that she ordered her to wait upon her periodically. The female barber noticed with no little concern the necklace round the queen's neck. The day of her second visit came on, and she instructed the elder of her two sons to set up a loud cry in the palace, and not to stop crying till he got into his hands the Duo queen's necklace. The female barber, accordingly, went again on the appointed day to the Duo queen's apartments. While she was engaged in painting the queen's feet, the elder boy set up a loud cry. On being asked the reason of the cry, the boy, as previously instructed, said that he wanted the queen's necklace. The queen said that it was impossible for her to part with that particular necklace, for it was the best and most valuable of all her jewels. To gratify the boy, however, she took it off her neck, and put it into the boy's hand. The boy stopped crying and held the necklace tight in his hand. As the female barber after she had done her work was about to go away, the queen wanted the necklace back. But the boy would not part with it. When his mother attempted to snatch it from him, he wept bitterly, and showed as if his heart would break. On which the female barber said—"Will your Majesty be gracious enough to let the boy take the necklace home with him? When he falls asleep after drinking his milk, which he is sure to do in the course of an hour, I will carefully bring it back to you." The queen, seeing that the boy would not allow it to be taken away from him, agreed to the proposal of the female barber, especially reflecting that Dalim, whose life depended on it, had long ago gone to the abodes of death.

Thus possessed of the treasure on which the life of her husband depended, the woman went with breathless haste to the garden-house and presented the necklace to Dalim, who had been restored to life. Their joy knew no bounds, and by the advice of their friend they determined the next day to go to the palace in state, and present themselves to the king and the Suo queen. Due preparations were made; an elephant, richly caparisoned, was brought for the prince Dalim Kumar, a pair of ponies for the two little boys, and a *chaturdala*[6] furnished with curtains of gold lace for the princess. Word was sent to the king and the Suo queen that the prince Dalim Kumar was not only alive, but that he was coming to visit his royal parents with his wife and sons. The king and Suo queen could hardly believe in the report, but being assured of its truth they were entranced with joy; while the Duo queen, anticipating the disclosure of all her wiles, became overwhelmed with grief. The procession of Dalim Kumar, which was attended by a band of musicians, approached the palace-gate; and the king and Suo queen went out to receive their long-lost son. It is needless to say that their joy was intense. They fell on each other's neck and wept. Dalim then related all the circumstances connected with his death. The king, inflamed with rage, ordered the Duo queen into his presence. A large hole, as deep as the height of a man, was dug in the ground. The Duo queen was put into it in a standing posture. Prickly thorn was heaped around her up to the crown of her head; and in this manner she was buried alive.

Thus my story endeth,
The Natiya-thorn withereth;
"Why, O Natiya-thorn, dost wither?"
"Why does thy cow on me browse?"
"Why, O cow, dost thou browse?"

"Why does thy neat-herd not tend me?"
"Why, O neat-herd, dost not tend the cow?"
"Why does thy daughter-in-law not give me rice?"
"Why, O daughter-in-law, dost not give rice?"
"Why does my child cry?"
"Why, O child, dost thou cry?"
"Why does the ant bite me?"
"Why, O ant, dost thou bite?"
Koot! koot! koot!

1. Kings, in Bengali folk-tales, have invariably two queens—the elder is called duo, that is, not loved; and the younger is called suo, that is, loved.
2. Dalim or dadimba means a pomegranate, and kumara son.
3. Bidhata-Purusha is the deity that predetermines all the events of the life of man or woman, and writes on the forehead of the child, on the sixth day of its birth, a brief precis of them.
4. There are eight forms of marriage spoken of in the Hindu Sastras, of which the Gandharva is one, consisting in the exchange of garlands.
5. Alakta is leaves or flimsy paper saturated with lac.
6. A sort of open Palki, used generally for carrying the bridegroom and bride in marriage processions.

2

Phakir Chand

here was a king's son, and there was a minister's son. They loved each other dearly; they sat together, they stood up together, they walked together, they ate together, they slept together, they got up together. In this way they spent many years in each other's company, till they both felt a desire to see foreign lands. So one day they set out on their journey. Though very rich, the one being the son of a king and the other the son of his chief minister, they did not take any servants with them; they went by themselves on horseback. The horses were beautiful to look at; they were *pakshirajes*, or kings of birds. The king's son and the minister's son rode together many days. They passed through extensive plains covered with paddy; through cities, towns, and villages; through waterless, treeless deserts; through dense forests which were the abode of the tiger and the bear. One evening they were overtaken by night in a region where human habitations were not seen; and as it was getting darker and darker, they dismounted beneath a lofty tree, tied their horses to its trunk, and, climbing up, sat on its branches covered with thick foliage. The tree grew near a large tank, the water of which was as clear as the eye of a crow. The king's son and the minister's son made themselves as comfortable as they could on the tree, being determined to spend on its branches the livelong night. They sometimes chatted together in whispers on account of the lonely terrors of the region; they sometimes sat demurely silent for some minutes; and anon they were falling into a doze, when their attention was arrested by a terrible sight.

A sound like the rush of many waters was heard from the middle of the tank. A huge serpent was seen leaping up from under the water with its hood of enormous size. It "lay floating many a rood"; then it swam ashore, and went about hissing. But what most of all attracted the attention of the king's son and the minister's son was a brilliant *manikya* (jewel) on the crested hood of the serpent. It shone like a thousand diamonds. It lit up the tank, its embankments, and the objects round about. The serpent doffed the jewel from its crest and threw it on the ground, and then it went about hissing in search of food. The two friends sitting on the tree greatly admired the wonderful brilliant, shedding ineffable lustre on everything around. They had never before seen anything like it; they had only heard of it as equalling the treasures of seven kings. Their admiration, however, was soon changed into sorrow and fear; for the serpent came hissing to the foot of the tree on the branches of which they were seated, and swallowed up, one by one, the horses tied to the trunk. They feared that they themselves would be the next victims, when, to their infinite relief, the gigantic cobra turned away from the tree, and went about roaming to a great distance. The minister's son, seeing this, bethought himself of taking possession of the lustrous stone. He had heard that the only way to hide the brilliant light of the jewel was to cover it with cow-dung or horse-dung, a quantity of which latter article he perceived lying at the foot of the tree. He came down from the tree softly, picked up the horse-dung, threw it upon the precious stone, and again climbed into the tree. The serpent, not perceiving the light of its head-jewel, rushed with great fury to the spot where it had been left. Its hissings, groans, and convulsions were terrible. It went round and round the jewel covered with horse-dung, and then breathed its last. Early next morning the king's son and the minister's son alighted from the tree, and went to the spot where the crest-jewel was. The mighty serpent lay there perfectly lifeless. The minister's son took up in his hand the jewel covered with horse-dung; and both of them went to the tank to wash it. When all the horse-dung had been washed off, the jewel shone as brilliantly as before. It lit up the entire bed of the tank, and exposed to their view the innumerable fishes swimming about in the waters. But what was their astonishment when they saw, by the light of the jewel, in the bottom of the tank, the lofty walls of what seemed a magnificent palace. The venturesome son of the minister proposed to the prince that they should dive into the waters and get at the palace below. They both dived into the waters—the jewel being in the hand of the minister's son—and in a moment stood at the gate of the palace. The gate was open. They saw no being, human or superhuman. They went inside the gate, and saw a beautiful garden laid out on the ample grounds round about the house which was in the centre. The king's son and the minister's son had never seen such a profusion of flowers. The rose with its many varieties, the jessamine, the *bel*, the *mallika*, the king of smells, the lily of the valley, the *Champaka*, and a thousand other sorts of sweet-scented flowers were there. And of each of these flowers there seemed to be a large number. Here were a hundred rose-bushes, there many acres covered with the delicious jessamine, while yonder were extensive plantations of all sorts of flowers. As all the plants were begemmed with flowers, and as the flowers were in full bloom, the air was loaded with rich perfume. It was a wilderness of sweets. Through this paradise of perfumery they proceeded towards the house, which was surrounded by banks of lofty trees. They stood at the door of the house. It was a fairy palace. The walls were of burnished gold, and here and there shone diamonds of dazzling hue which were stuck into the walls. They did not meet with any beings, human or other. They went inside, which was richly furnished. They went from room to room, but they did not see any one. It seemed to be a deserted house. At last, however, they found in one room a young lady lying down, apparently in sleep, on a bed of golden framework. She was of exquisite beauty; her complexion was a mixture of red and white; and her age was apparently about sixteen. The king's son and the minister's son gazed upon her with rapture; but they had not stood long when this young lady of superb beauty opened her eyes, which seemed like those of a gazelle. On seeing the strangers she said: "How have you come here, ye unfortunate men? Begone, begone! This is the abode of a mighty serpent, which has devoured my father, my mother, my brothers, and all my relatives; I am the only one of my family that he has spared. Flee for your lives, or else the serpent will put you both in its capacious maw." The minister's son told the princess how the serpent had breathed its last; how he and his friend had got possession of its head-jewel, and by its light had come to her palace. She thanked the strangers for delivering her from the infernal serpent, and begged of them to live in the house, and never to desert her. The king's son and the minister's son gladly accepted the invitation. The king's son, smitten with the charms of the peerless princess, married her after a short time; and as there was no priest there, the hymeneal knot was tied by a simple exchange of garlands of flowers.

The king's son became inexpressibly happy in the company of the princess, who was as amiable in her disposition as she was beautiful in her person; and though the wife of the minister's son was living in the upper world, he too participated in his friend's happiness.

"She took up the jewel in her hand, left the palace, and successfully reached the upper world"

Time thus passed merrily, when the king's son bethought himself of returning to his native country; and as it was fit that he should go with his princess in due pomp, it was determined that the minister's son should first ascend from the subaqueous regions, go to the king, and bring with him attendants, horses, and elephants for the happy pair. The snake-jewel was therefore had in requisition. The prince, with the jewel in hand, accompanied the minister's son to the upper world, and bidding adieu to his friend returned to his lovely wife in the enchanted palace. Before leaving, the minister's son appointed the day and the hour when he would stand on the high embankments of the tank with horses, elephants, and attendants, and wait upon the prince and the princess, who were to join him in the upper world by means of the jewel.

Leaving the minister's son to wend his way to his country and to make preparations for the return of his king's son, let us see how the happy couple in the subterranean palace were passing their time. One day, while the prince was sleeping after his noonday meal, the princess, who had never seen the upper regions, felt the desire of visiting them, and the rather as the snake-jewel, which alone could give her safe conduct through the waters, was at that moment shedding its bright effulgence in the room. She took up the jewel in her hand, left the palace, and successfully reached the upper world. No mortal caught her sight. She sat on the flight of steps with which the tank was furnished for the convenience of bathers, scrubbed her body, washed her hair, disported in the waters, walked about on the water's edge, admired all the scenery around, and returned to her palace, where she found her husband still locked in the embrace of sleep. When the prince woke up, she did not tell him a word about her adventure. The following day at the same hour, when her husband was asleep, she paid a second visit to the upper world, and went back unnoticed by mortal man.

As success made her bold, she repeated her adventure a third time. It so chanced that on that day the son of the Rajah, in whose territories the tank was situated, was out on a hunting excursion, and had pitched his tent not far from the place. While his attendants were engaged in cooking their noon-day meal, the Rajah's son sauntered about on the embankments of the tank, near which an old woman was gathering sticks and dried branches of trees for purposes of fuel. It was while the Rajah's son and the old woman were near the tank that the princess paid her third visit to the upper world. She rose up from the waters, gazed around, and seeing a man and a woman on the banks again went down. The Rajah's son caught a momentary glimpse of the princess, and so did the old woman gathering sticks. The Rajah's son stood gazing on the waters. He had never seen such a beauty. She seemed to him to be one of those *deva-kanyas*, heavenly goddesses, of whom he had read in old books, and who are said now and then to favour the lower world with their visits, which, like angel visits, are "few and far between." The unearthly beauty of the princess, though he had seen her only for a moment, made a deep impression on his heart, and distracted his mind. He stood there like a statue, for hours, gazing on the waters, in the hope of seeing the lovely figure again. But in vain. The princess did not appear again. The Rajah's son became mad with love. He kept muttering— "Now here, now gone! Now here, now gone!" He would not leave the place till he was forcibly removed by the attendants who had now come to him. He was taken to his father's palace in a state of hopeless insanity. He spoke to nobody; he always sobbed heavily; and the only words which proceeded out of his mouth—and he was muttering them every minute—were, "Now here, now gone! Now here, now gone!" The Rajah's grief may well be conceived. He could not imagine what should have deranged his son's mind. The words, "Now here, now gone," which ever and anon issued from his son's lips, were a mystery to him; he could not unravel their meaning; neither could the attendants throw any light on the subject. The best physicians of the country were consulted, but to no effect. The sons of Æsculapius could not ascertain the cause of the madness, far less could they cure it. To the many inquiries of the physicians, the only reply made by the Rajah's son was the stereotyped words—"Now here, now gone! Now here, now gone!"

The Rajah, distracted with grief on account of the obscuration of his son's intellects, caused a proclamation to be made in the capital by beat of drum, to the effect that, if any person could explain the cause of his son's madness and cure it, such a person would be rewarded with the hand of the Rajah's daughter, and with the possession of half his kingdom. The drum was beaten round most parts of the city, but no one touched it, as no one knew the cause of the madness of the Rajah's son. At last an old woman touched the drum, and declared that she would not only discover the cause of the madness, but cure it. This woman, who was the identical woman that was gathering sticks near the tank at the time the Rajah's son lost his reason, had a crack-brained son of the name of Phakir Chand, and was in consequence called Phakir's mother, or more familiarly Phakre's mother. When the woman was brought before the Rajah, the following conversation took place:—

Rajah. You are the woman that touched the drum.—You know the cause of my son's madness?

Phakir's Mother. Yes, O incarnation of justice! I know the cause, but I will not mention it till I have cured your son.

Rajah. How can I believe that you are able to cure my son, when the best physicians of the land have failed?

Phakir's Mother. You need not now believe, my lord, till I have performed the cure. Many an old woman knows secrets with which wise men are unacquainted.

Rajah. Very well, let me see what you can do. In what time will you perform the cure?

Phakir's Mother. It is impossible to fix the time at present; but I will begin work immediately with your lordship's assistance.

Rajah. What help do you require from me?

Phakir's Mother. Your lordship will please order a hut to be raised on the embankment of the tank where your son first caught the disease. I mean to live in that hut for a few days. And your lordship will also please order some of your servants to be in attendance at a distance of about a hundred yards from the hut, so that they might be within call.

Rajah. Very well; I will order that to be immediately done. Do you want anything else?

Phakir's Mother. Nothing else, my lord, in the way of preparations. But it is as well to remind your lordship of the conditions on which I undertake the cure. Your lordship has promised to give to the performer of the cure the hand of your daughter and half your kingdom. As I am a woman and cannot marry your daughter, I beg that, in case I perform the cure, my son Phakir Chand may marry your daughter and take possession of half your kingdom.

Rajah. Agreed, agreed.

A temporary hut was in a few hours erected on the embankment of the tank, and Phakir's mother took up her abode in it. An outpost was also erected at some distance for servants in attendance who might be required to give help to the woman. Strict orders were given by Phakir's mother that no human being should go near the tank excepting herself. Let us leave Phakir's mother keeping watch at the tank, and hasten down into the subterranean palace to see what the prince and the princess are about. After the mishap which had occurred on her last visit to the upper world, the princess had given up the idea of a fourth visit. But women generally have greater curiosity than men; and the princess of the underground palace was no exception to the general rule. One day, while her husband was asleep as usual after his noonday meal, she rushed out of the palace with the snake-jewel in her hand, and came to the upper world. The moment the upheaval of the waters in the middle of the tank took place, Phakir's mother, who was on the alert, concealed herself in the hut and began looking through the chinks of the matted wall. The princess, seeing no mortal near, came to the bank, and sitting there began to scrub her body. Phakir's mother showed herself outside the hut, and addressing the princess, said in a winning tone—"Come, my child, thou queen of beauty, come to me, and I will help you to bathe." So saying, she approached the princess, who, seeing that it was only a woman, made no resistance. The old woman, while in the act of washing the hair of the princess, noticed the bright jewel in her hand, and said—"Put the jewel here till you are bathed." In a moment the jewel was in the possession of Phakir's mother, who wrapped it up in the cloth that was round her waist. Knowing the princess to be unable to escape, she gave the signal to the attendants in waiting, who rushed to the tank and made the princess a captive.

Great were the rejoicings of the people when the tidings reached the city that Phakir's mother had captured a water-nymph from the nether regions. The whole city came to see the "daughter of the immortals," as they called the princess. When she was brought to the palace and confronted with the Rajah's son of obscured intellect, the latter said with a shout of exultation—"I have found! I have found!" The cloud which had settled on his brain was dissipated in a moment. The eyes, erewhile vacant and lustreless, now glowed with the fire of intelligence; his tongue, of which he had almost lost the use—the only words which he used to utter being, "Now here, now gone!"—was now relaxed: in a word, he was restored to his senses. The joy of the Rajah knew no bounds. There was great festivity in the city; and the people who showered benedictions on the head of Phakir Chand's mother, expected the speedy celebration of the marriage of the Rajah's son with the beauty of the nether world. The princess, however, told the Rajah, through Phakir's mother, that she had made a vow to the effect that she would not, for one whole year, look at the face of another man than that of her husband who was dwelling beneath the waters, and that therefore the marriage could not be performed during that period. Though the Rajah's son was somewhat disappointed, he readily agreed to the delay, believing, agreeably to the proverb, that delay would greatly enhance the sweetness of those pleasures which were in store for him.

It is scarcely necessary to say that the princess spent her days and her nights in sorrowing and sighing. She lamented that idle curiosity which had led her to come to the upper world, leaving her husband below. When she recollected that her husband was all alone below the waters she wept bitter tears. She wished she could run away. But that was impossible, as she was immured within walls, and there were walls within walls. Besides, if she could get out of the palace and of the city, of what avail would it be? She could not gain her husband, as the serpent jewel was not in her possession. The ladies of the palace and Phakir's mother tried to divert her mind, but in vain. She took pleasure in nothing; she would hardly speak to any one; she wept day and night. The year of her vow was drawing to a close, and yet she was disconsolate. The marriage, however, must be celebrated. The Rajah consulted the astrologers, and the day and the hour in which the nuptial knot was to be tied were fixed. Great preparations were made. The confectioners of the city busied themselves day and night in preparing sweetmeats; milkmen took contracts for supplying the palace with tanks of curds; gunpowder was being manufactured for a grand display of fireworks; bands of musicians were placed on sheds erected over the palace gate, who ever and anon sent forth many "a bout of linked sweetness"; and the whole city assumed an air of mirth and festivity.

It is time we should think of the minister's son, who, leaving his friend in the subterranean palace, had gone to his country to bring horses, elephants, and attendants for the return of the king's son and his lovely princess with due pomp. The preparations took him many months; and when everything was ready he started on his journey, accompanied by a long train of elephants, horses, and attendants. He reached the tank two or three days before the appointed day. Tents were pitched in the mango-topes adjoining the tank for the accommodation of men and cattle; and the minister's son always kept his eyes fixed on the tank. The sun of the appointed day sank below the horizon; but the prince and the princess dwelling beneath the waters made no sign. He waited two or three days longer; still the prince did not make his appearance. What could have happened to his friend and his beautiful wife? Were they dead? Had another serpent, possibly the mate of the one that had died, beaten the prince and the princess to death? Had they somehow lost the serpent-jewel? Or had they been captured when they were once on a visit to the upper world? Such were the reflections of the minister's son. He was overwhelmed with grief. Ever since he had come to the tank he had heard at regular intervals the sound of music coming from the city which was not distant. He inquired of passers-by what that music meant. He was told that the Rajah's son was about to be married to some wonderful young lady, who had come out of the waters of that very tank on the bank of which he was now seated, and that the marriage ceremony was to be performed on the day following the next. The minister's son immediately concluded that the wonderful young lady of the lake that was to be married was none other than the wife of his friend, the king's son. He resolved therefore to go into the city to learn the details of the affair, and try if possible to rescue the princess. He told the attendants to go home, taking with them the elephants and the horses; and he himself went to the city, and took up his abode in the house of a Brahman.

After he had rested and taken his dinner, the minister's son asked the Brahman what the meaning was of the music that was heard in the city at regular intervals. The Brahman asked, "From what part of the world have you come that you have not heard of the wonderful circumstance that a young lady of heavenly beauty rose out of the waters of a tank in the suburbs, and that she is going to be married the day after to-morrow to the son of our Rajah?"

Minister's Son. No, I have heard nothing. I have come from a distant country whither the story has not reached. Will you kindly tell me the particulars?

Brahman. The Rajah's son went out a-hunting about this time last year. He pitched his tents close to a tank in the suburbs. One day, while the Rajah's son was walking near the tank, he saw a young woman, or rather goddess, of uncommon beauty rise from the waters of the tank. She gazed about for a minute or two and disappeared. The Rajah's son, however, who had seen her, was so struck with her heavenly beauty that he became desperately enamoured of her. Indeed, so intense was his passion, that his reason gave way; and he was carried home hopelessly mad. The only words he uttered day and night were—"Now here, now gone!" The Rajah sent for all the best physicians of the country for restoring his son to his reason; but the physicians were powerless. At last he caused a proclamation to be made by beat of drum to the effect that if any one could cure the Rajah's son, he should be the Rajah's son-in-law and the owner of half his kingdom. An old woman, who went by the name of Phakir's mother, took hold of the drum, and declared her ability to cure the Rajah's son. On the tank where the princess had appeared was raised for Phakir's mother a hut in which she took up her abode; and not far from her hut another hut was erected for the accommodation of attendants who might be required to help her. It seems the goddess rose from the waters; Phakir's mother seized her with the help of the attendants, and carried her in a palki to the palace. At the sight of her the Rajah's son was restored to his senses; and the marriage would have been celebrated at that time but for a vow which the goddess had made that she would not look at the face of any male person till the lapse of a year. The year of the vow is now over; and the music which you have heard is from the gate of the Rajah's palace. This, in brief, is the story.

Minister's Son. A truly wonderful story! And has Phakir's mother, or rather Phakir Chand himself, been rewarded with the hand of the Rajah's daughter and with the possession of half the kingdom?

Brahman. No, not yet. Phakir has not been got hold of. He is a half-witted lad, or rather quite mad. He has been away for more than a year from his home, and no one knows where he is. That is his manner; he stays away for a long time, suddenly comes home, and again disappears. I believe his mother expects him soon.

Minister's Son. What like is he? and what does he do when he returns home?

Brahman. Why, he is about your height, though he is somewhat younger than you. He puts on a small piece of cloth round his waist, rubs his body with ashes, takes the branch of a tree in his hand, and, at the door of the hut in which his mother lives, dances to the tune of *dhoop! dhoop! dhoop*! His articulation is very indistinct; and when his mother says—"Phakir! stay with me for some days," he invariably answers in his usual unintelligible manner, "No, I won't remain, I won't remain." And when he wishes to give an affirmative answer, he says, "Hoom," which means "Yes."

The above conversation with the Brahman poured a flood of light into the mind of the minister's son. He saw how matters stood. He perceived that the princess of the subterranean palace must have alone ventured out into the tank by means of the snake-jewel; that she must have been captured alone without the king's son; that the snake-jewel must be in the possession of Phakir's mother; and that his friend, the king's son, must be alone below the waters without any means of escape. The desolate and apparently hopeless state of his friend filled him with unutterable grief. He was in deep musings during most part of the night. Is it impossible, thought he, to rescue the king's son from the nether regions? What if, by some means or other, I contrive to get the jewel from the old woman? And can I not do it by personating Phakir Chand himself, who is expected by his mother shortly? And possibly by the same means I may be able to rescue the princess from the Rajah's palace. He resolved to act the rôle of Phakir Chand the following day. In the morning he left the Brahman's house, went to the outskirts of the city, divested himself of his usual clothing, put round his waist a short and narrow piece of cloth which scarcely reached his knee-joints, rubbed his body well with ashes, took in his hand a twig which he broke off a tree, and thus accoutred, presented himself before the door of the hut of Phakir's mother. He commenced operations by dancing, in a most violent manner, to the tune of *dhoop! dhoop! dhoop!* The dancing attracted the notice of the old woman, who, supposing that her son had come, said—"My son Phakir, are you come? Come, my darling; the gods have at last become propitious to us." The supposed Phakir Chand uttered the monosyllable "hoom," and went on dancing in a still more violent manner than before, waving the twig in his hand. "This time you must not go away," said the old woman, "you must remain with me." "No, I won't remain, I won't remain," said the minister's son. "Remain with me, and I'll get you married to the Rajah's daughter. Will you marry, Phakir Chand?" The minister's son replied—"Hoom, hoom," and danced on like a madman. "Will you come with me to the Rajah's house? I'll show you a princess of uncommon beauty who has risen from the waters." "Hoom, hoom," was the answer that issued from his lips, while his feet tripped it violently to the sound of *dhoop! dhoop!* "Do you wish to see a manik, Phakir, the crest jewel of the serpent, the treasure of seven kings?" "Hoom, hoom," was the reply. The old woman brought out of the hut the snake-jewel, and put it into the hand of her supposed son. The minister's son took it, and carefully wrapped it up in the piece of cloth round his waist. Phakir's mother, delighted beyond measure at the opportune appearance of her son, went to the Rajah's house, partly to announce to the Rajah the news of Phakir's appearance, and partly to show Phakir the princess of the waters. The supposed Phakir and his mother found ready access to the Rajah's palace, for the old woman had, since the capture of the princess, become the most important person in the kingdom. She took him into the room where the princess was, and introduced him to her. It is superfluous to remark that the princess was by no means pleased with the company of a madcap, who was in a state of semi-nudity, whose body was rubbed with ashes, and who was ever and anon dancing in a wild manner. At sunset the old woman proposed to her son that they should leave the palace and go to their own house. But the supposed Phakir Chand refused to comply with the request; he said he would stay there that night. His mother tried to persuade him to return with her, but he persisted in his determination. He said he would remain with the princess. Phakir's mother therefore went away, after giving instructions to the guards and attendants to take care of her son.

When all in the palace had retired to rest, the supposed Phakir, coming towards the princess, said in his own usual voice—"Princess! do you not recognise me? I am the minister's son, the friend of your princely husband." The princess, astonished at the announcement, said—"Who? The minister's son? Oh, my husband's best friend, do rescue me from this terrible captivity, from this worse than death. O fate! it is by my own fault that I am reduced to this wretched state. Oh, rescue me, rescue me, thou best of friends!" She then burst into tears. The minister's son said, "Do not be disconsolate. I will try my best to rescue you this very night; only you must do whatever I tell you." "I will do anything you tell me, minister's son; anything you tell me." After this the supposed Phakir left the room, and passed through the courtyard of the palace. Some of the guards challenged him, to whom he replied, "Hoom, hoom; I will just go out for a minute and again come in presently." They understood that it was the madcap Phakir. True to his word he did come back shortly, and went to the princess. An hour afterwards he again went out and was again challenged, on which he made the same reply as at the first time. The guards

who challenged him began to mutter between their teeth—
"This madcap of a Phakir will, we suppose, go out and come
in all night. Let the fellow alone; let him do what he likes.
Who can be sitting up all night for him?" The minister's son
was going out and coming in with the view of accustoming the
guards to his constant egress and ingress, and also of watching
for a favourable opportunity to escape with the princess. About
three o'clock in the morning the minister's son again passed
through the courtyard, but this time no one challenged him,
as all the guards had fallen asleep. Overjoyed at the auspicious
circumstance, he went to the princess. "Now, princess, is
the time for escape. The guards are all asleep. Mount on
my back, and tie the locks of your hair round my neck, and
keep tight hold of me." The princess did as she was told. He
passed unchallenged through the courtyard with the lovely
burden on his back, passed out of the gate of the palace—no
one challenging him, passed on to the outskirts of the city,
and reached the tank from which the princess had risen. The
princess stood on her legs, rejoicing at her escape, and at the
same time trembling. The minister's son untied the snake-jewel
from his waist-cloth, and descending into the waters, both
he and she found their way to the subterranean palace. The
reception which the prince in the subaqueous palace gave to his
wife and his friend may be easily imagined. He had nearly died
of grief; but now he suffered a resurrection. The three were now
mad with joy. During the three days that they remained in the
palace they again and again told the story of the egress of the
princess into the upper world, of her seizure, of her captivity in
the palace, of the preparations for marriage, of the old woman,
of the minister's son personating Phakir Chand, and of the
successful deliverance. It is unnecessary to add that the prince

and the princess expressed their gratitude to the minister's son in the warmest terms, declared him to be their best and greatest friend, and vowed to abide always, till the day of their death, by his advice, and to follow his counsel.

Being resolved to return to their native country, the king's son, the minister's son, and the princess left the subterranean palace, and, lighted in the passage by the snake-jewel, made their way good to the upper world. As they had neither elephants nor horses, they were under the necessity of travelling on foot; and though this mode of travelling was troublesome to both the king's son and the minister's son, as they were bred in the lap of luxury, it was infinitely more troublesome to the princess, as the stones of the rough road

> *"Wounded the invisible*
> *Palms of her tender feet where'er they fell."*

When her feet became very sore, the king's son sometimes took her up on his broad shoulders, on which she sat astride; but the load, however lovely, was too heavy to be carried any great distance. She therefore, for the most part, travelled on foot.

One evening they bivouacked beneath a tree, as no human habitations were visible. The minister's son said to the prince and princess, "Both of you go to sleep, and I will keep watch in order to prevent any danger." The royal couple were soon locked in the arms of sleep. The faithful son of the minister did not sleep, but sat up watching. It so happened that on that tree swung the nest of the two immortal birds, Bihangama and

Bihangami, who were not only endowed with the power of human speech, but who could see into the future. To the no little astonishment of the minister's son the two prophetical birds joined in the following conversation:—

Bihangama. The minister's son has already risked his own life for the safety of his friend, the king's son; but he will find it difficult to save the prince at last.

Bihangami. Why so?

Bihangama. Many dangers await the king's son. The prince's father, when he hears of the approach of his son, will send for him an elephant, some horses, and attendants. When the king's son rides on the elephant he will fall down and die.

Bihangami. But suppose some one prevents the king's son from riding on the elephant, and makes him ride on horseback, will he not in that case be saved?

Bihangama. Yes, he will in that case escape that danger, but a fresh danger awaits him. When the king's son is in sight of his father's palace, and when he is in the act of passing through its lion-gate, the lion-gate will fall upon him and crush him to death.

Bihangami. But suppose some one destroys the lion-gate before the king's son goes up to it; will not the king's son in that case be saved?

Bihangama. Yes, in that case he will escape that particular danger; but a fresh danger awaits him. When the king's son reaches the palace and sits at a feast prepared for him, and when he takes into his mouth the head of a fish cooked for him, the head of the fish will stick in his throat and choke him to death.

Bihangami. But suppose some one sitting at the feast

snatches the head of the fish from the prince's plate, and thus prevents him from putting it into his mouth, will not the king's son in that case be saved?

Bihangama. Yes, in that case he will escape that particular danger; but a fresh danger awaits him. When the prince and princess after dinner retire into their sleeping apartment, and they lie together in bed, a terrible cobra will come into the room and bite the king's son to death.

Bihangami. But suppose some one lying in wait in the room cut the snake into pieces, will not the king's son in that case be saved?

Bihangama. Yes, in that case the life of the king's son will be saved; but if the man who kills the snake repeats to the king's son the conversation between you and me, that man will be turned into a marble statue.

Bihangami. But is there no means of restoring the marble statue to life?

Bihangama. Yes, the marble statue may be restored to life if it is washed with the life-blood of the infant which the princess will give birth to, immediately after it is ushered into the world.

The conversation of the prophetical birds had extended thus far when the crows began to caw, the east put on a reddish hue, and the travellers beneath the tree bestirred themselves. The conversation stopped, but the minister's son had heard it all.

The prince, the princess, and the minister's son pursued their journey in the morning; but they had not walked many hours when they met a procession consisting of an elephant, a horse, a *palki*, and a large number of attendants. These animals and men had been sent by the king, who had heard that his son, together with his newly married wife and his friend the minister's son, were not far from the capital on their journey homewards. The elephant, which was richly caparisoned, was intended for the prince; the *palki* the framework of which was silver and was gaudily adorned, was meant for the princess; and the horse for the minister's son. As the prince was about to mount on the elephant, the minister's son went up to him and said—"Allow me to ride on the elephant, and you please ride on horseback." The prince was not a little surprised at the coolness of the proposal. He thought his friend was presuming too much on the services he had rendered; he was therefore nettled, but remembering that his friend had saved both him and his wife, he said nothing, but quietly mounted the horse, though his mind became somewhat alienated from him. The procession started, and after some time came in sight of the palace, the lion-gate of which had been gaily adorned for the reception of the prince and the princess. The minister's son told the prince that the lion-gate should be broken down before the prince could enter the palace. The prince was astounded at the proposal, especially as the minister's son gave no reasons for so extraordinary a request. His mind became still more estranged from him; but in consideration of the services the minister's son had rendered, his request was complied with, and the beautiful lion-gate, with its gay decorations, was broken down.

"He rushed out of his hiding-place and killed the serpent"

The party now went into the palace, where the king gave a warm reception to his son, to his daughter-in-law, and to the minister's son. When the story of their adventures was related, the king and his courtiers expressed great astonishment, and they all with one voice extolled the sagacity, prudence, and devotedness of the minister's son. The ladies of the palace were struck with the extraordinary beauty of the new-comer; her complexion was milk and vermilion mixed together; her neck was like that of a swan; her eyes were like those of a gazelle; her lips were as red as the berry *bimba*; her cheeks were lovely; her nose was straight and high; her hair reached her ankles; her walk was as graceful as that of a young elephant—such were the terms in which the connoisseurs of beauty praised the princess whom destiny had brought into the midst of them. They sat around her and put her a thousand questions regarding her parents, regarding the subterranean palace in which she formerly lived, and the serpent which had killed all her relatives. It was now time that the new arrivals should have their dinner. The dinner was served up in dishes of gold. All sorts of delicacies were there, amongst which the most conspicuous was the large head of a *rohita* fish placed in a golden cup near the prince's plate. While they were eating, the minister's son suddenly snatched the head of the fish from the prince's plate, and said, "Let me, prince, eat this rohita's head." The king's son was quite indignant. He said nothing, however. The minister's son perceived that his friend was in a terrible rage; but he could not help it, as his conduct, however strange, was necessary to the safety of his friend's life; neither could he clear himself by stating the reason of his behaviour, as in that case he himself would be transformed into a marble statue. The dinner over, the minister's son expressed his desire to go to his own house. At other times the king's son would not allow his friend to go away in that fashion; but being shocked at his strange conduct, he readily agreed to the proposal. The minister's son, however, had not the slightest notion of going to his own house; he was resolved to avert the last peril that was to threaten the life of his friend. Accordingly, with a sword in his hand, he stealthily entered the room in which the prince and the princess were to sleep that night, and ensconced himself under the bedstead, which was furnished with mattresses of down and canopied with mosquito curtains of the richest silk and gold lace. Soon after dinner the prince and princess came into the bedroom, and undressing themselves went to bed. At midnight, while the royal couple were asleep, the minister's son perceived a snake of gigantic size enter the room through one of the water-passages, and climb up the tester-frame of the bed. He rushed out of his hiding-place, killed the serpent, cut it up in pieces, and put the pieces in the dish for holding betel-leaves and spices. It so happened, however, that as the minister's son was cutting the serpent into pieces, a drop of blood fell on the breast of the princess, and the rather as the mosquito curtains had not been let down. Thinking that the drop of blood might injure the fair princess, he resolved to lick it up. But as he regarded it as a great sin to look upon a young woman lying asleep half naked, he blindfolded himself with seven-fold cloth, and licked up the drop of blood. But while he was in the act of licking it, the princess awoke and screamed, and her scream roused her husband lying beside her. The prince seeing the minister's son, who he thought had gone away to his own house, bending over the body of his wife, fell into a great rage, and would have got up and killed him, had not the minister's son besought him to restrain his anger, adding—"Friend, I have done this only in order to save your life." "I do not understand what you mean," said the prince; "ever since we came out of the subterranean palace you have been behaving in a most extraordinary way. In the first place, you prevented me from getting upon the richly caparisoned elephant, though my father, the king, had purposely sent it for me. I thought, however, that a sense of the services you had rendered to me had made you exceedingly vain; I therefore let the matter pass, and mounted the horse. In the second place, you insisted on the destruction of the fine lion-gate, which my father had adorned with gay decorations; and I let that matter also pass. Then, again, at dinner you snatched away, in a most shameful manner, the rohita's head which was on my plate, and devoured it yourself, thinking, no doubt, that you were entitled to higher honours than I. You then pretended that you were going home, for which I was not at all sorry, as you had made yourself very disagreeable to me. And now you are actually in my bedroom, bending over the naked bosom of my wife. You must have had some evil design; and you pretend that you have done this to save my life. I fancy it was not for saving my life, but for destroying my wife's chastity." "Oh, do not harbour such thoughts in your mind against me. The gods know that I have done all this for the preservation of your life. You would see the reasonableness of my conduct throughout if I had the liberty of stating my reasons." "And why are you not at liberty?" asked the prince; "who has shut up your mouth?" "It is destiny that has shut up my mouth," answered the minister's son; "if I were to tell it all, I should be transformed into a marble statue." "You would be transformed into a marble statue!" exclaimed the prince; "you must take me to be a simpleton to believe this nonsense." "Do you wish me then, friend," said the minister's son, "to tell you all? You must then make up your mind to see your friend turned into stone." "Come, out with it," said the prince, "or else you are a dead man." The minister's son, in order to clear himself of the foul accusation brought against him, deemed it his duty to reveal the secret at the risk of his life. He again and again warned the prince not to press him. But the prince remained inexorable. The minister's son then went on to say that, while bivouacking under a lofty tree one night, he had overheard a conversation between Bihangama and Bihangami, in which the former predicted all the dangers that were to threaten the life of the prince. When the minister's son had related the prediction concerning the mounting upon the elephant, his lower parts were turned into stone. He then, turning to the prince, said, "See, friend, my lower parts have already turned into stone." "Go on, go on," said the prince, "with your story." The minister's son then related the prophecy regarding the destruction of the lion-gate, when half of his body was converted into stone. He then related the prediction regarding the eating of the head of the fish, when his body up to his neck was petrified. "Now, friend," said the minister's son, "the whole of my body, excepting my neck and head, is petrified; if I tell the rest, I shall assuredly become a man of stone. Do you wish me still to go on?" "Go on," answered the prince, "go on." "Very well, I will go on to the end," said the minister's son; "but in case you repent after I have become turned into stone, and wish me to be restored to life, I will tell you of the manner in which it may be effected. The princess after a few months will be delivered of a child; if immediately after the birth of the infant you kill it and besmear my marble body with its blood, I shall be restored to life." He then related the prediction regarding the serpent in the bedroom; and when the last word was on his lips the rest of his body was turned into stone, and he dropped on the floor a marble image. The princess jumped out of bed, opened the vessel for betel-leaves and spices, and saw there pieces of a serpent. Both the prince and the princess now became convinced of the good faith and benevolence of their departed friend. They went to the marble figure, but it was lifeless. They set up a loud lamentation; but it was to no purpose, for the marble moved not. They then resolved to keep the marble figure concealed in a safe place, and to besmear it with the blood of their first-born child when it should be ushered into existence.

In process of time the hour of the princess's travail came on, and she was delivered of a beautiful boy, the perfect image of his mother. Both father and mother were struck with the beauty of their child, and would fain have spared its life; but recollecting the vows they had made on behalf of their best friend, now lying in a corner of the room a lifeless stone, and the inestimable services he had rendered to both of them, they cut the child into two, and besmeared the marble figure of the minister's son with its blood. The marble became animated in a moment. The minister's son stood before the prince and princess, who became exceedingly glad to see their old friend again in life. But the minister's son, who saw the lovely new-born babe lying in a pool of blood, was overwhelmed with grief. He took up the dead infant, carefully wrapped it up in a towel, and resolved to get it restored to life.

The minister's son, intent on the reanimation of his friend's child, consulted all the physicians of the country; but they said that they would undertake to cure any person of any disease so long as life was in him, but when life was extinct, the case was beyond their jurisdiction. The minister's son at last bethought himself of his own wife, who was living in a distant town, and who was a devoted worshipper of the goddess Kali, who, through his wife's intercession, might be prevailed upon to give life to the dead child. He, accordingly, set out on a journey to the town in which his wife was living in her father's house. Adjoining that house there was a garden where upon a tree he hung the dead child wrapped up in a towel. His wife was overjoyed to see her husband after so long a time; but to her surprise she found that he was very melancholy, that he spoke very little, and that he was brooding over something in his mind. She asked the reason of his melancholy, but he kept quiet. One night while they were lying together in bed, the wife got up and opening the door went out. The husband, who had little sleep any night in consequence of the weight of anxiety regarding the reanimation of his friend's child, perceiving his wife go out at that dead hour of night, determined to follow her without being noticed. She went to a temple of the goddess Kali, which was at no great distance from her house. She worshipped the goddess with flowers and sandal-wood perfume, and said, "O mother Kali! have mercy upon me, and deliver me out of all my troubles." The goddess replied, "Why, what further grievance have you? You long prayed for the return of your husband, and he has returned; what aileth thee now?" The woman answered, "True, O Mother, my husband has come to me, but he is very moody and melancholy, hardly speaks to me, takes no delight in me, only sits moping in a corner." To which the goddess rejoined, "Ask your husband what the reason of his melancholy is, and let me know it." The minister's son overheard the conversation between the goddess and his wife, but he did not make his appearance; he quietly slunk away before his wife and went to bed. The following day the wife asked her husband of the cause of his melancholy; and he related all the particulars regarding the killing of the infant child of the prince. Next night at the same dead hour the wife proceeded to Kali's temple and mentioned to the goddess the reason of her husband's melancholy; on which the goddess said, "Bring the child here and I will restore it to life." On the succeeding night the child was produced before the goddess Kali, and she called it back to life. Entranced with joy, the minister's son took up the reanimated child, went as fast as his legs could carry him to the prince and princess, and presented to them their child alive and well. They all rejoiced with exceeding great joy, and lived together happily till the day of their death.

3

The Indigent Brahman

There was a Brahman who had a wife and four children. He was very poor. With no resources in the world, he lived chiefly on the benefactions of the rich. His gains were considerable when marriages were celebrated or funeral ceremonies were performed; but as his parishioners did not marry every day, neither did they die every day, he found it difficult to make the two ends meet. His wife often rebuked him for his inability to give her adequate support, and his children often went about naked and hungry. But though poor he was a good man. He was diligent in his devotions; and there was not a single day in his life in which he did not say his prayers at stated hours. His tutelary deity was the goddess Durga, the consort of Siva, the creative Energy of the Universe. On no day did he either drink water or taste food till he had written in red ink the name of Durga at least one hundred and eight times; while throughout the day he incessantly uttered the ejaculation, "O Durga! O Durga! have mercy upon me." Whenever he felt anxious on account of his poverty and his inability to support his wife and children, he groaned out— "Durga! Durga! Durga!"

One day, being very sad, he went to a forest many miles distant from the village in which he lived, and indulging his grief wept bitter tears. He prayed in the following manner:—"O Durga! O Mother Bhagavati! wilt thou not make an end of my misery? Were I alone in the world, I should not have been sad on account of poverty; but thou hast given me a wife and children. Give me, O Mother, the means to support them." It so happened that on that day and on that very spot the god Siva and his wife Durga were taking their morning walk. The goddess Durga, on seeing the Brahman at a distance, said to her divine husband—"O Lord of Kailas! do you see that Brahman? He is always taking my name on his lips and offering the prayer that I should deliver him out of his troubles. Can we not, my lord, do something for the poor Brahman, oppressed as he is with the cares of a growing family? We should give him enough to make him comfortable. As the poor man and his family have never enough to eat, I propose that you give him a *handi*[1] which should yield him an inexhaustible supply of *mudki*."[2] The lord of Kailas readily agreed to the proposal of his divine consort, and by his decree created on the spot a handi possessing the required quality. Durga then, calling the Brahman to her, said,—"O Brahman! I have often thought of your pitiable case. Your repeated prayers have at last moved my compassion. Here is a handi for you. When you turn it upside down and shake it, it will pour down a never-ceasing shower of the finest mudki, which will not end till you restore the handi to its proper position. Yourself, your wife, and your children can eat as much mudki as you like, and you can also sell as much as you like." The Brahman, delighted beyond measure at obtaining so inestimable a treasure, made obeisance to the goddess, and, taking the handi in his hand, proceeded towards his house as fast as his legs could carry him. But he had not gone many yards when he thought of testing the efficacy of the wonderful vessel. Accordingly he turned the handi upside down and shook it, when, lo, and behold! a quantity of the finest mudki he had ever seen fell to the ground. He tied the sweetmeat in his sheet and walked on. It was now noon, and the Brahman was hungry; but he could not eat without his ablutions and his prayers. As he saw in the way an inn, and not far from it a tank, he purposed to halt there that he might bathe, say his prayers, and then eat the much-desired mudki. The Brahman sat at the innkeeper's shop, put the handi near him, smoked tobacco, besmeared his body with mustard oil, and before proceeding to bathe in the adjacent tank gave the handi in charge to the innkeeper, begging him again and again to take especial care of it.

When the Brahman went to his bath and his devotions, the innkeeper thought it strange that he should be so careful as to the safety of his earthen vessel. There must be something valuable in the handi, he thought, otherwise why should the Brahman take so much thought about it? His curiosity being excited he opened the handi, and to his surprise found that it contained nothing. What can be the meaning of this? thought the innkeeper within himself. Why should the Brahman care so much for an empty handi? He took up the vessel, and began to examine it carefully; and when, in the course of examination, he turned the handi upside down, a quantity of the finest mudki fell from it, and went on falling without intermission. The innkeeper called his wife and children to witness this unexpected stroke of good fortune. The showers of the sugared fried paddy were so copious that they filled all the vessels and jars of the innkeeper. He resolved to appropriate to himself this precious handi, and accordingly put in its place another handi of the same size and make. The ablutions and devotions of the Brahman being now over, he came to the shop in wet clothes reciting holy texts of the Vedas. Putting on dry clothes, he wrote on a sheet of paper the name of Durga one hundred and eight times in red ink; after which he broke his fast on the mudki his handi had already given him. Thus refreshed, and being about to resume his journey homewards, he called for his handi, which the innkeeper delivered to him, adding—"There, sir, is your handi; it is just where you put it; no one has touched it." The Brahman, without suspecting anything, took up the handi and proceeded on his journey; and as he walked on, he congratulated himself on his singular good fortune. "How agreeably," he thought within himself, "will my poor wife be surprised! How greedily the children will devour the mudki of heaven's own manufacture! I shall soon become rich, and lift up my head with the best of them all." The pains of travelling were considerably alleviated by these joyful anticipations. He reached his house, and calling his wife and children, said— "Look now at what I have brought. This handi that you see is an unfailing source of wealth and contentment. You will see what a stream of the finest mudki will flow from it when I turn it upside down." The Brahman's good wife, hearing of mudki falling from the handi unceasingly, thought that her husband must have gone mad; and she was confirmed in her opinion when she found that nothing fell from the vessel though it was turned upside down again and again. Overwhelmed with grief, the Brahman concluded that the innkeeper must have played a trick with him; he must have stolen the handi Durga had given him, and put a common one in its stead. He went back the next day to the innkeeper, and charged him with having changed his handi. The innkeeper put on a fit of anger, expressed surprise at the Brahman's impudence in charging him with theft, and drove him away from his shop.

"Instead of sweetmeats about a score of demons"

The Brahman then bethought himself of an interview with the goddess Durga who had given him the handi, and accordingly went to the forest where he had met her. Siva and Durga again favoured the Brahman with an interview. Durga said—"So, you have lost the handi I gave you. Here is another, take it and make good use of it." The Brahman, elated with joy, made obeisance to the divine couple, took up the vessel, and went on his way.

He had not gone far when he turned it upside down, and shook it in order to see whether any mudki would fall from it. Horror of horrors! instead of sweetmeats about a score of demons, of gigantic size and grim visage, jumped out of the handi, and began to belabour the astonished Brahman with blows, fisticuffs and kicks. He had the presence of mind to turn up the handi and to cover it, when the demons forthwith disappeared. He concluded that this new handi had been given him only for the punishment of the innkeeper. He accordingly went to the innkeeper, gave him the new handi in charge, begged of him carefully to keep it till he returned from his ablutions and prayers. The innkeeper, delighted with this second godsend, called his wife and children, and said—"This is another handi brought here by the same Brahman who brought the handi of mudki. This time, I hope, it is not mudki but sandesa.[3] Come, be ready with baskets and vessels, and I'll turn the handi upside down and shake it." This was no sooner done than scores of fierce demons started up, who caught hold of the innkeeper and his family and belaboured them mercilessly. They also began upsetting the shop, and would have completely destroyed it, if the victims had not besought the Brahman, who had by this time returned from his ablutions, to show mercy to them and send away the terrible demons. The Brahman acceded to the innkeeper's request, he dismissed the demons by shutting up the vessel; he got the former handi, and with the two handis went to his native village.

On reaching home the Brahman shut the door of his house, turned the mudki-handi upside down, and shook it; the result was an unceasing stream of the finest mudki that any confectioner in the country could produce. The man, his wife, and their children devoured the sweetmeat to their hearts' content; all the available earthen pots and pans of the house were filled with it; and the Brahman resolved the next day to turn confectioner, to open a shop in his house, and sell mudki. On the very day the shop was opened, the whole village came to the Brahman's house to buy the wonderful mudki. They had never seen such mudki in their life, it was so sweet, so white, so large, so luscious; no confectioner in the village or any town in the country had ever manufactured anything like it. The reputation of the Brahman's mudki extended, in a few days, beyond the bounds of the village, and people came from remote parts to purchase it. Cartloads of the sweetmeat were sold every day, and the Brahman in a short time became very rich. He built a large brick house, and lived like a nobleman of the land. Once, however, his property was about to go to wreck and ruin. His children one day by mistake shook the wrong handi, when a large number of demons dropped down and caught hold of the Brahman's wife and children and were striking them mercilessly, when happily the Brahman came into the house and turned up the handi. In order to prevent a similar catastrophe in future, the Brahman shut up the demon-handi in a private room to which his children had no access.

Pure and uninterrupted prosperity, however, is not the lot of mortals; and though the demon-handi was put aside, what security was there that an accident might not befall the mudki-handi? One day, during the absence of the Brahman and his wife from the house, the children decided upon shaking the handi; but as each of them wished to enjoy the pleasure of shaking it there was a general struggle to get it, and in the mêlée the handi fell to the ground and broke. It is needless to say that the Brahman, when on reaching home he heard of the disaster, became inexpressibly sad. The children were of course well cudgelled, but no flogging of children could replace the magical handi. After some days he again went to the forest, and offered many a prayer for Durga's favour. At last Siva and Durga again appeared to him, and heard how the handi had been broken. Durga gave him another handi, accompanied with the following caution—"Brahman, take care of this handi; if you again break it or lose it, I'll not give you another." The Brahman made obeisance, and went away to his house at one stretch without halting anywhere. On reaching home he shut the door of his house, called his wife to him, turned the handi upside down, and began to shake it. They were only expecting mudki to drop from it, but instead of mudki a perennial stream of beautiful sandesa issued from it. And such sandesa! No confectioner of Burra Bazar ever made its like. It was more the food of gods than of men. The Brahman forthwith set up a shop for selling sandesa, the fame of which soon drew crowds of customers from all parts of the country. At all festivals, at all marriage feasts, at all funeral celebrations, at all Pujas, no one bought any other sandesa than the Brahman's. Every day, and every hour, many jars of gigantic size, filled with the delicious sweetmeat, were sent to all parts of the country.

The wealth of the Brahman excited the envy of the Zemindar of the village, who, having heard that the sandesa was not manufactured but dropped from a handi, devised a plan for getting possession of the miraculous vessel. At the celebration of his son's marriage he held a great feast, to which were invited hundreds of people. As many mountain-loads of sandesa would be required for the purpose, the Zemindar proposed that the Brahman should bring the magical handi to the house in which the feast was held. The Brahman at first refused to take it there; but as the Zemindar insisted on its being carried to his own house, he reluctantly consented to take it there. After many Himalayas of sandesa had been shaken out, the handi was taken possession of by the Zemindar, and the Brahman was insulted and driven out of the house. The Brahman, without giving vent to anger in the least, quietly went to his house, and taking the demon-handi in his hand, came back to the door of the Zemindar's house. He turned the handi upside down and shook it, on which a hundred demons started up as from the vasty deep and enacted a scene which it is impossible to describe. The hundreds of guests that had been bidden to the feast were caught hold of by the unearthly visitants and beaten; the women were dragged by their hair from the Zenana and dashed about amongst the men; while the big and burly Zemindar was driven about from room to room like a bale of cotton. If the demons had been allowed to do their will only for a few minutes longer, all the men would have been killed, and the very house razed to the ground. The Zemindar fell prostrate at the feet of the Brahman and begged for mercy. Mercy was shown him, and the demons were removed. After that the Brahman was no more disturbed by the Zemindar or by any one else; and he lived many years in great happiness and enjoyment.

1. Handi is an earthen pot, generally used in cooking food.
2. Mudki, fried paddy boiled dry in treacle or sugar.
3. A sort of sweetmeat made of curds and sugar.

4

The Story of the Rakshasas

There was a poor half-witted Brahman who had a wife but no children. It was only with difficulty he could supply the wants of himself and his wife. And the worst of it was that he was rather lazily inclined. He was averse to taking long journeys, otherwise he might always have had enough, in the shape of presents from rich men, to enable him and his wife to live comfortably. There was at that time a king in a neighbouring country who was celebrating the funeral obsequies of his mother with great pomp. Brahmans and beggars were going from different parts with the expectation of receiving rich presents. Our Brahman was requested by his wife to seize this opportunity and get a little money; but his constitutional indolence stood in the way. The woman, however, gave her husband no rest till she extorted from him the promise that he would go. The good woman, accordingly, cut down a plantain tree and burnt it to ashes, with which ashes she cleaned the clothes of her husband, and made them as white as any fuller could make them. She did this because her husband was going to the palace of a great king, who could not be approached by men clothed in dirty rags; besides, as a Brahman, he was bound to appear neat and clean. The Brahman at last one morning left his house for the palace of the great king. As he was somewhat imbecile, he did not inquire of any one which road he should take; but he went on and on, and proceeded whithersoever his two eyes directed him. He was of course not on the right road, indeed he had reached a region where he did not meet with a single human being for many miles, and where he saw sights which he had never seen in his life. He saw hillocks of cowries (shells used as money) on the roadside: he had not proceeded far from them when he saw hillocks of pice, then successively hillocks of four-anna pieces, hillocks of eight-anna pieces, and hillocks of rupees. To the infinite surprise of the poor Brahman, these hillocks of shining silver coins were succeeded by a large hill of burnished gold-mohurs, which were all as bright as if they had been just issued from the mint. Close to this hill of gold-mohurs was a large house which seemed to be the palace of a powerful and rich king, at the door of which stood a lady of exquisite beauty. The lady, seeing the Brahman, said, "Come, my beloved husband; you married me when I was young, and you never came once after our marriage, though I have been daily expecting you. Blessed be this day which has made me see the face of my husband. Come, my sweet, come in, wash your feet and rest after the fatigues of your journey; eat and drink, and after that we shall make ourselves merry." The Brahman was astonished beyond measure. He had no recollection of having been married in early youth to any other woman than the woman who was now keeping house with him. But being a Kulin Brahman, he thought it was quite possible that his father had got him married when he was a little child, though the fact had made no impression on his mind. But whether he remembered it or not, the fact was certain, for the woman declared that she was his wedded wife,—and such a wife! as beautiful as the goddesses of Indra's heaven, and no doubt as wealthy as she was beautiful. While these thoughts were passing through the Brahman's mind, the lady said again, "Are you doubting in your mind whether I am your wife? Is it possible that all recollection of that happy event has been effaced from your mind—all the pomp and circumstance of our nuptials? Come in, beloved; this is your own house, for whatever is mine is thine." The Brahman succumbed to the loving entreaties of the fair lady, and went into the house. The house was not an ordinary one—it was a magnificent palace, all the apartments being large and lofty and richly furnished. But one thing surprised the Brahman very much, and that was that there was no other person in the house besides the lady herself. He could not account for so singular a phenomenon; neither could he explain how it was that he did not meet with any human being in his morning and evening walks. The fact was that the lady was not a human being. She was a Rakshasi.[1] She had eaten up the king, the queen, and all the members of the royal family, and gradually all his subjects. This was the reason why human beings were not seen in those parts.

"At the door of which stood a lady of exquisite beauty"

The Rakshasi and the Brahman lived together for about a week, when the former said to the latter, "I am very anxious to see my sister, your other wife. You must go and fetch her, and we shall all live together happily in this large and beautiful house. You must go early to-morrow, and I will give you clothes and jewels for her." Next morning the Brahman, furnished with fine clothes and costly ornaments, set out for his home. The poor woman was in great distress; all the Brahmans and Pandits that had been to the funeral ceremony of the king's mother had returned home loaded with largesses; but her husband had not returned,—and no one could give any news of him, for no one had seen him there. The woman therefore concluded that he must have been murdered on the road by highwaymen. She was in this terrible suspense, when one day she heard a rumour in the village that her husband was seen coming home with fine clothes and costly jewels for his wife. And sure enough the Brahman soon appeared with his valuable load. On seeing his wife the Brahman thus accosted her:—"Come with me, my dearest wife; I have found my first wife. She lives in a stately palace, near which are hillocks of rupees and a large hill of gold-mohurs. Why should you pine away in wretchedness and misery in this horrible place? Come with me to the house of my first wife, and we shall all live together happily." When the woman heard her husband speak of his first wife, of hillocks of rupees and of a hill of gold-mohurs, she thought in her mind that her half-witted good man had become quite mad; but when she saw the exquisitely beautiful silks and satins and the ornaments set with diamonds and precious stones, which only queens and princesses were in the habit of putting on, she concluded in her mind that her poor husband had fallen into the meshes of a Rakshasi. The Brahman, however, insisted on his wife's going with him, and declared that if she did not come she was at liberty to pine away in poverty, but that for himself he meant to return forthwith to his first and rich wife. The good woman, after a great deal of altercation with her husband, resolved to go with him and judge for herself how matters stood. They set out accordingly the next morning, and went by the same road on which the Brahman had travelled. The woman was not a little surprised to see hillocks of cowries, of pice, of eight-anna pieces, of rupees, and last of all a lofty hill of gold-mohurs. She saw also an exceedingly beautiful lady coming out of the palace hard by, and hastening towards her. The lady fell on the neck of the Brahman woman, wept tears of joy, and said, "Welcome, beloved sister! this is the happiest day of my life! I have seen the face of my dearest sister!" The party then entered the palace.

What with the stately mansion in which he was lodged, with the most delectable provisions which seemed to rise as if by enchantment, what with the caresses and endearments of his two wives, the one human and the other demoniac, who vied with each other in making him happy and comfortable, the Brahman had a jolly time of it. He was steeped as it were in an ocean of enjoyment. Some fifteen or sixteen years were spent by the Brahman in this state of Elysian pleasure, during which period his two wives presented him with two sons. The Rakshasi's son, who was the elder, and who looked more like a god than a human being, was named Sahasra Dal, literally the Thousand-Branched; and the son of the Brahman woman, who was a year younger, was named Champa Dal, that is, branch of a champaka tree. The two boys loved each other dearly. They were both sent to a school which was several miles distant, to which they used every day to go riding on two little ponies of extraordinary fleetness.

The Brahman woman had all along suspected from a thousand little circumstances that her sister-in-law was not a human being but a Rakshasi; but her suspicion had not yet ripened into certainty, for the Rakshasi exercised great self-restraint on herself, and never did anything which human beings did not do. But the demoniac nature, like murder, will out. The

Brahman having nothing to do, in order to pass his time had recourse to hunting. The first day he returned from the hunt, he had bagged an antelope. The antelope was laid in the courtyard of the palace. At the sight of the antelope the mouth of the raw-eating Rakshasi began to water. Before the animal was dressed for the kitchen, she took it away into a room, and began devouring it. The Brahman woman, who was watching the whole scene from a secret place, saw her Rakshasi sister tear off a leg of the antelope, and opening her tremendous jaws, which seemed to her imagination to extend from earth to heaven, swallow it up. In this manner the body and other limbs of the antelope were devoured, till only a little bit of the meat was kept for the kitchen. The second day another antelope was bagged, and the third day another; and the Rakshasi, unable to restrain her appetite for raw flesh, devoured these two as she had devoured the first. On the third day the Brahman woman expressed to the Rakshasi her surprise at the disappearance of nearly the whole of the antelope with the exception of a little bit. The Rakshasi looked fierce and said, "Do I eat raw flesh?" To which the Brahman woman replied, "Perhaps you do, for aught I know to the contrary." The Rakshasi, knowing herself to be discovered, looked fiercer than before, and vowed revenge. The Brahman woman concluded in her mind that the doom of herself, of her husband, and of her son was sealed. She spent a miserable night, believing that next day she would be killed and eaten up, and that her husband and son would share the same fate. Early next morning, before her son Champa Dal went to school, she gave him in a small golden vessel a little quantity of her own breast milk, and told him to be constantly watching its colour. "Should you," she said, "see the milk get a little red, then conclude that your father has been killed; and should you see it grow still redder, then conclude that I am killed: when you see this, gallop away for your life as fast as your horse can carry you, for if you do not, you also will be devoured."

The Rakshasi on getting up from bed—and she had prevented the Brahman overnight from having any communication with his wife—proposed that she and the Brahman should go to bathe in the river, which was at some distance. She would take no denial; the Brahman had therefore to follow her as meekly as a lamb. The Brahman woman at once saw from the proposal that ruin was impending; but it was beyond her power to avert the catastrophe. The Rakshasi, on the river-side, assuming her own proper gigantic dimensions, took hold of the ill-fated Brahman, tore him limb by limb, and devoured him up. She then ran to her house, and seized the Brahman woman, and put her into her capacious stomach, clothes, hair and all. Young Champa Dal, who, agreeably to his mother's instructions, was diligently watching the milk in the small golden vessel, was horror-struck to find the milk redden a little. He set up a cry and said that his father was killed; a few minutes after, finding the milk become completely red, he cried yet louder, and rushing to his pony, mounted it. His half-brother, Sahasra Dal, surprised at Champa Dal's conduct, said, "Where are you going, Champa? Why are you crying? Let me accompany you." "Oh! do not come to me. Your mother has devoured my father and mother; don't you come and devour me." "I will not devour you; I'll save you." Scarcely had he uttered these words and galloped away after Champa Dal, when he saw his mother in her own Rakshasi form appearing at a distance, and demanding that Champa Dal should come to her. He said,

"I will come to you, not Champa." So saying, he went to his mother, and with his sword, which he always wore as a young prince, cut off her head.

Champa Dal had, in the meantime, galloped off a good distance, as he was running for his life; but Sahasra Dal, by pricking his horse repeatedly, soon overtook him, and told him that his mother was no more. This was small consolation to Champa Dal, as the Rakshasi, before being killed, had devoured both his father and mother; still he could not but feel that Sahasra Dal's friendship was sincere. They both rode fast, and as their horses were of the breed of pakshirajes (literally, kings of birds), they travelled over hundreds of miles. An hour or two before sundown they descried a village, to which they made up, and became guests in the house of one of its most respectable inhabitants. The two friends found the members of that respectable family in deep gloom. Evidently there was something agitating them very much. Some of them held private consultations, and others were weeping. The eldest lady of the house, the mother of its head, said aloud, "Let me go, as I am the eldest. I have lived long enough; at the utmost my life would be cut short only by a year or two." The youngest member of the house, who was a little girl, said, "Let me go, as I am young and useless to the family; if I die I shall not be missed." The head of the house, the son of the old lady, said, "I am the head and representative of the family; it is but reasonable that I should give up my life." His younger brother said, "You are the main prop and pillar of the family; if you go the whole family is ruined. It is not reasonable that you should go; let me go, as I shall not be much missed." The two strangers listened to all this conversation with no little curiosity. They wondered what it all meant. Sahasra Dal at last, at the risk of being thought meddlesome, ventured to ask the head of the house the subject of their consultations, and the reason of the deep misery but too visible in their countenances and words. The head of the house gave the following answer: "Know then, worthy guests, that this part of the country is infested by a terrible Rakshasi, who has depopulated all the regions round. This town, too, would have been depopulated, but that our king became a suppliant before the Rakshasi, and begged her to show mercy to us his subjects. The Rakshasi replied, 'I will consent to show mercy to you and to your subjects only on this condition, that you every night put a human being, either male or female, in a certain temple for me to feast upon. If I get a human being every night I will rest satisfied, and not commit any further depredations on your subjects.' Our king had no other alternative than to agree to this condition, for what human beings can ever hope to contend against a Rakshasi? From that day the king made it a rule that every family in the town should in its turn send one of its members to the temple as a victim to appease the wrath and to satisfy the hunger of the terrible Rakshasi. All the families in this neighbourhood have had their turn, and this night it is the turn for one of us to devote himself to destruction. We are therefore discussing who should go. You must now perceive the cause of our distress." The two friends consulted together for a few minutes, and at the conclusion of their consultations, Sahasra Dal, who was the spokesman of the party, said, "Most worthy host, do not any longer be sad: as you have been very kind to us, we have resolved to requite your hospitality by ourselves going to the temple and becoming the food of the Rakshasi. We go as your representatives." The whole family protested against the proposal. They declared that guests were like gods, and that it was the duty of the host to endure all sorts of privation for the comfort of the guest, and not the duty of the guest to suffer for the host. But the two strangers insisted on standing proxy to the family, who, after a great deal of yea and nay, at last consented to the arrangement.

Immediately after candle-light, Sahasra Dal and Champa Dal, with their two horses, installed themselves in the temple, and shut the door. Sahasra told his brother to go to sleep, as he himself was determined to sit up the whole night and watch against the coming of the terrible Rakshasi. Champa was soon in a fine sleep, while Sahasra lay awake. Nothing happened during the early hours of the night, but no sooner had the gong of the king's palace announced the dead hour of midnight than Sahasra heard the sound as of a rushing tempest, and immediately concluded, from his knowledge of Rakshasas, that the Rakshasi was nigh. A thundering knock was heard at the door, accompanied with the following words:—

> *"How, mow, khow!*
> *A human being I smell;*
> *Who watches inside?"*

To this question Sahasra Dal made the following reply:—
> *"Sahasra Dal watcheth,*
> *Champa Dal watcheth,*
> *Two winged horses watch."*

On hearing this answer the Rakshasi turned away with a groan, knowing that Sahasra Dal had Rakshasa blood in his veins. An hour after, the Rakshasi returned, thundered at the door, and called out—

> *"How, mow, khow!*
> *A human being I smell;*
> *Who watcheth inside?"*

Sahasra Dal again replied—

> *"Sahasra Dal watcheth,*
> *Champa Dal watcheth,*
> *Two winged horses watch."*

The Rakshasi again groaned and went away. At two o'clock and at three o'clock the Rakshasi again and again made her appearance, and made the usual inquiry, and obtaining the same answer, went away with a groan. After three o'clock, however, Sahasra Dal felt very sleepy: he could not any longer keep awake. He therefore roused Champa, told him to watch, and strictly enjoined upon him, in reply to the query of the Rakshasi, to mention Sahasra's name first. With these instructions he went to sleep. At four o'clock the Rakshasi again made her appearance, thundered at the door, and said—

> *"How, mow, khow!*
> *A human being I smell;*
> *Who watches inside?"*

As Champa Dal was in a terrible fright, he forgot the instructions of his brother for the moment, and answered—

> *"Champa Dal watcheth,*
> *Sahasra Dal watcheth,*
> *Two winged horses watch."*

On hearing this reply the Rakshasi uttered a shout of exultation, laughed such a laugh as only demons can, and with a dreadful noise broke open the door. The noise roused Sahasra, who in a moment sprung to his feet, and with his sword, which was as supple as a palm-leaf, cut off the head of the Rakshasi. The huge mountain of a body fell to the ground, making a great noise, and lay covering many an acre. Sahasra Dal kept the severed head of the Rakshasi near him, and went to sleep. Early in the morning some wood-cutters, who were passing near the temple, saw the huge body on the ground. They could not from a distance make out what it was, but on coming near they knew that it was the carcase of the terrible Rakshasi, who had by her voracity nearly depopulated the country. Remembering the promise made by the king that the killer of the Rakshasi should be rewarded by the hand of his daughter and with a share of the kingdom, each of the wood-cutters, seeing no claimant at hand, thought of obtaining the reward. Accordingly each of them cut off a part of a limb of the huge carcase, went to the king, and represented himself to be the destroyer of the great raw-eater, and claimed the reward. The king, in order to find out the real hero and deliverer, inquired of his minister the name of the family whose turn it was on the preceding night to offer a victim to the Rakshasi. The head of that family, on being brought before the king, related how two youthful travellers, who were guests in his house, volunteered to go into the temple in the room of a member of his family. The door of the temple was broken open; Sahasra Dal and Champa Dal and their horses were found all safe; and the head of the Rakshasi, which was with them, proved beyond the shadow of a doubt that they had killed the monster. The king kept his word. He gave his daughter in marriage to Sahasra Dal and the sovereignty of half his dominions. Champa Dal remained with his friend in the king's palace, and rejoiced in his prosperity.

Sahasra Dal and Champa Dal lived together happily for some time, when a misunderstanding arose between them in this wise. There was in the service of the queen-mother a certain maid-servant who was the most useful domestic in the palace. There was nothing which she could not put her hands to and perform. She had uncommon strength for a woman; neither was her intelligence of a mean order. She was a woman of immense activity and energy; and if she were absent one day from the palace, the affairs of the zenana would be in perfect disorder. Hence her services were highly valued by the queen-mother and all the ladies of the palace. But this woman was not a woman; she was a Rakshasi, who had put on the appearance of a woman to serve some purposes of her own, and then taken service in the royal household. At night, when every one in the palace was asleep, she used to assume her own real form, and go about in quest of food, for the quantity of food that is sufficient for either man or woman was not sufficient for a Rakshasi. Now Champa Dal, having no wife, was in the habit of sleeping outside the zenana, and not far from the outer gate of the palace.

"In a trice she woke up, sat up in her bed, and eyeing the stranger, inquired who he was"

He had noticed her going about on the premises and devouring sundry goats and sheep, horses and elephants. The maidservant, finding that Champa Dal was in the way of her supper, determined to get rid of him. She accordingly went one day to the queen-mother, and said, "Queen-mother! I am unable any longer to work in the palace." "Why? what is the matter, Dasi?[2] How can I get on without you? Tell me your reasons. What ails you?" "Why," said the woman, "nowadays it is impossible for a poor woman like me to preserve my honour in the palace. There is that Champa Dal, the friend of your son-in-law; he always cracks indecent jokes with me. It is better for me to beg for my rice than to lose my honour. If Champa Dal remains in the palace I must go away." As the maid-servant was an absolute necessity in the palace, the queen-mother resolved to sacrifice Champa Dal to her. She therefore told Sahasra Dal that Champa Dal was a bad man, that his character was loose, and that therefore he must leave the palace. Sahasra Dal earnestly pleaded on behalf of his friend, but in vain; the queen-mother had made up her mind to drive him out of the palace. Sahasra Dal had not the courage to speak personally to his friend on the subject; he therefore wrote a letter to him, in which he simply said that for certain reasons Champa must leave the palace immediately. The letter was put in his room after he had gone to bathe. On reading the letter Champa Dal, exceedingly grieved, mounted his fleet horse and left the palace.

As Champa's horse was uncommonly fleet, in a few hours he traversed thousands of miles, and at last found himself at the gateway of what seemed a magnificent palace. Dismounting from his horse, he entered the house, where he did not meet with a single creature. He went from apartment to apartment, but though they were all richly furnished he did not see a single human being. At last, in one of the side rooms, he found a young lady of heavenly beauty lying down on a splendid bedstead. She was asleep. Champa Dal looked upon the sleeping beauty with rapture—he had not seen any woman so beautiful. Upon the bed, near the head of the young lady, were two sticks, one of silver and the other of gold. Champa took the silver stick into his hand, and touched with it the body of the lady; but no change was perceptible. He then took up the gold stick and laid it upon the lady, when in a trice she woke up, sat in her bed, and eyeing the stranger, inquired who he was. Champa Dal briefly told his story. The young lady, or rather princess—for she was nothing less—said, "Unhappy man! why have you come here? This is the country of Rakshasas, and in this house and round about there live no less than seven hundred Rakshasas. They all go away to the other side of the ocean every morning in search of provisions; and they all return every evening before dusk. My father was formerly king in these regions, and had millions of subjects, who lived in flourishing towns and cities. But some years ago the invasion of the Rakshasas took place, and they devoured all his subjects, and himself and my mother, and my brothers and sisters. They devoured also all the cattle of the country. There is no living human being in these regions excepting myself; and I too should long ago have been devoured had not an old Rakshasi, conceiving strange affection for me, prevented the other Rakshasas from eating me up. You see those sticks of silver and gold; the old Rakshasi, when she goes away in the morning, kills me with the silver stick, and on her return in the evening re-animates me with the gold stick. I do not know how to advise you; if the Rakshasas see you, you are a dead man." Then they both talked to each other in a very affectionate manner, and laid their heads together to devise if possible some means of escape from the hands of the Rakshasas. The hour of the return of the seven hundred raw-eaters was fast approaching; and Keshavati—for that was the name of the princess, so called from the abundance of her hair—told Champa to hide himself in the heaps of the sacred trefoil which were lying in the temple of Siva in the central part of the palace. Before Champa went to his place of concealment, he touched Keshavati with the silver stick, on which she instantly died.

Shortly after sunset Champa Dal heard from beneath the heaps of the sacred trefoil the sound as of a mighty rushing wind. Presently he heard terrible noises in the palace. The Rakshasas had come home from cruising, after having filled their stomachs, each one, with sundry goats, sheep, cows, horses, buffaloes, and elephants. The old Rakshasi, of whom we have already spoken, came to Keshavati's room, roused her by touching her body with the gold stick, and said—

> *"Hye, mye, khye!*
> *A human being I smell."*

On which Keshavati said, "I am the only human being here; eat me if you like." To which the raw-eater replied, "Let me eat up your enemies; why should I eat you?" She laid herself down on the ground, as long and as high as the Vindhya Hills, and presently fell asleep. The other Rakshasas and Rakshasis also soon fell asleep, being all tired out on account of their gigantic labours in the day. Keshavati also composed herself to sleep; while Champa, not daring to come out of the heaps of leaves, tried his best to court the god of repose. At daybreak all the raw-eaters, seven hundred in number, got up and went as usual to their hunting and predatory excursions, and along with them went the old Rakshasi, after touching Keshavati with the silver stick. When Champa Dal saw that the coast was clear, he came out of the temple, walked into Keshavati's room, and touched her with the gold stick, on which she woke up. They sauntered about in the gardens, enjoying the cool breeze of the morning; they bathed in a lucid tank which was in the grounds; they ate and drank, and spent the day in sweet converse. They concocted a plan for their deliverance. They settled that Keshavati should ask the old Rakshasi on what the life of a Rakshasa depended, and when the secret should be made known they would adopt measures accordingly. As on the preceding evening, Champa, after touching his fair friend with the silver stick, took refuge in the temple beneath the heaps of the sacred trefoil. At dusk the Rakshasas as usual came home; and the old Rakshasi, rousing her pet, said—

"Hye, mye, khye!
A human being I smell."

Keshavati answered, "What other human being is here excepting myself? Eat me up, if you like." "Why should I eat you, my darling? Let me eat up all your enemies." Then she laid down on the ground her huge body, which looked like a part of the Himalaya mountains. Keshavati, with a phial of heated mustard oil, went towards the feet of the Rakshasi, and said, "Mother, your feet are sore with walking; let me rub them with oil." So saying, she began to rub with oil the Rakshasi's feet; and while she was in the act of doing so, a few tear-drops from her eyes fell on the monster's leg. The Rakshasi smacked the tear-drops with her lips, and finding the taste briny, said, "Why are you weeping, darling? What aileth thee?" To which the princess replied, "Mother, I am weeping because you are old, and when you die I shall certainly be devoured by one of the Rakshasas." "When I die! Know, foolish girl, that we Rakshasas never die. We are not naturally immortal, but our life depends on a secret which no human being can unravel. Let me tell you what it is that you may be comforted. You know yonder tank; there is in the middle of it a Sphatikasthambha,[3] on the top of which in deep waters are two bees. If any human being can dive into the waters, and bring up to land the two bees from the pillar in one breath, and destroy them so that not a drop of their blood falls to the ground, then we Rakshasas shall certainly die; but if a single drop of blood falls to the ground, then from it will start up a thousand Rakshasas. But what human being will find out this secret, or, finding it, will be able to achieve the feat? You need not, therefore, darling, be sad; I am practically immortal." Keshavati treasured up the secret in her memory, and went to sleep.

Early next morning the Rakshasas as usual went away; Champa came out of his hiding-place, roused Keshavati, and fell a-talking. The princess told him the secret she had learnt from the Rakshasi. Champa immediately made preparations for accomplishing the mighty deed. He brought to the side of the tank a knife and a quantity of ashes. He disrobed himself, put a drop or two of mustard oil into each of his ears to prevent water from entering in, and dived into the waters. In a moment he got to the top of the crystal pillar in the middle of the tank, caught hold of the two bees he found there, and came up in one breath. Taking the knife, he cut up the bees over the ashes, a drop or two of the blood fell, not on the ground, but on the ashes. When Champa caught hold of the bees, a terrible scream was heard at a distance. This was the wailing of the Rakshasas, who were all running home to prevent the bees from being killed; but before they could reach the palace, the bees had perished. The moment the bees were killed, all the Rakshasas died, and their carcases fell on the very spot on which they were standing. Champa and the princess afterwards found that the gateway of the palace was blocked up by the huge carcases of the Rakshasas—some of them having nearly succeeded in getting to the palace. In this manner was effected the destruction of the seven hundred Rakshasas.

After the destruction of the seven hundred raw-eating monsters, Champa Dal and Keshavati got married together by the exchange of garlands of flowers. The princess, who had never been out of the house, naturally expressed a desire to see the outer world. They used every day to take long walks both morning and evening, and as a large river was hard by Keshavati wished to bathe in it. The first day they went to bathe, one of Keshavati's hairs came off, and as it is the custom with women never to throw away a hair unaccompanied with something else, she tied the hair to a shell which was floating on the water; after which they returned home. In the meantime the shell with the hair tied to it floated down the stream, and in course of time reached that ghat[4] at which Sahasra Dal and his companions were in the habit of performing their ablutions. The shell passed by when Sahasra Dal and his friends were bathing; and he, seeing it at some distance, said to them, "Whoever succeeds in catching hold of yonder shell shall be rewarded with a hundred rupees." They all swam towards it, and Sahasra Dal, being the fleetest swimmer, got it. On examining it he found a hair tied to it. But such hair! He had never seen so long a hair. It was exactly seven cubits long. "The owner of this hair must be a remarkable woman, and I must see her"— such was the resolution of Sahasra Dal. He went home from the river in a pensive mood, and instead of proceeding to the zenana for breakfast, remained in the outer part of the palace. The queen-mother, on hearing that Sahasra Dal was looking melancholy and had not come to breakfast, went to him and asked the reason. He showed her the hair, and said he must see the woman whose head it had adorned. The queen-mother said, "Very well, you shall have that lady in the palace as soon as possible. I promise you to bring her here." The queen-mother told her favourite maid-servant, whom she knew to be full of resources—the same who was a Rakshasi in disguise—that she must, as soon as possible, bring to the palace that lady who was the owner of the hair seven cubits long. The maid-servant said she would be quite able to fetch her. By her directions a boat was built of Hajol wood, the oars of which were of Mon Paban wood. The boat was launched on the stream, and she went on board of it with some baskets of wicker-work of curious workmanship; she also took with her some sweetmeats into which some poison had been mixed. She snapped her fingers thrice, and uttered the following charm:—

> *"Boat of Hajol!*
> *Oars of Mon Paban!*
> *Take me to the Ghat,*
> *In which Keshavati bathes."*

No sooner had the words been uttered than the boat flew like lightning over the waters. It went on and on, leaving behind many a town and city. At last it stopped at a bathing-place, which the Rakshasi maid-servant concluded was the bathing ghat of Keshavati. She landed with the sweetmeats in her hand. She went to the gate of the palace, and cried aloud, "O Keshavati! Keshavati! I am your aunt, your mother's sister. I am come to see you, my darling, after so many years. Are you in, Keshavati?" The princess, on hearing these words, came out of her room, and making no doubt that she was her aunt, embraced and kissed her. They both wept rivers of joy—at least the Rakshasi maid-servant did, and Keshavati followed suit through sympathy. Champa Dal also thought that she was the aunt of his newly married wife. They all ate and drank and took rest in the middle of the day. Champa Dal, as was his habit, went to sleep after breakfast. Towards afternoon, the supposed aunt said to Keshavati, "Let us both go to the river and wash ourselves." Keshavati replied, "How can we go now? my husband is sleeping." "Never mind," said the aunt, "let him sleep on; let me put these sweetmeats, that I have brought, near his bedside, that he may eat them when he gets up." They then went to the river-side close to the spot where the boat was. Keshavati, when she saw from some distance the baskets of wicker-work in the boat, said, "Aunt, what beautiful things are those! I wish I could get some of them." "Come, my child, come and look at them; and you can have as many as you like." Keshavati at first refused to go into the boat, but on being pressed by her aunt, she went. The moment they two were on board, the aunt snapped her fingers thrice and said:—

> *"Boat of Hajol!*
> *Oars of Mon Paban!*
> *Take me to the Ghat,*
> *In which Sahasra Dal bathes."*

As soon as these magical words were uttered the boat moved and flew like an arrow over the waters. Keshavati was frightened and began to cry, but the boat went on and on, leaving behind many towns and cities, and in a trice reached the ghat where Sahasra Dal was in the habit of bathing. Keshavati was taken to the palace; Sahasra Dal admired her beauty and the length of her hair; and the ladies of the palace tried their best to comfort her. But she set up a loud cry, and wanted to be taken back to her husband. At last when she saw that she was a captive, she told the ladies of the palace that she had taken a vow that she would not see the face of any strange man for six months. She was then lodged apart from the rest in a small house, the window of which overlooked the road; there she spent the livelong day and also the livelong night—for she had very little sleep—in sighing and weeping.

In the meantime when Champa Dal awoke from sleep, he was distracted with grief at not finding his wife. He now thought that the woman, who pretended to be his wife's aunt, was a cheat and an impostor, and that she must have carried away Keshavati. He did not eat the sweetmeats, suspecting they might be poisoned. He threw one of them to a crow which, the moment it ate it, dropped down dead. He was now the more confirmed in his unfavourable opinion of the pretended aunt. Maddened with grief, he rushed out of the house, and determined to go whithersoever his eyes might lead him. Like a madman, always blubbering "O Keshavati! O Keshavati!" he travelled on foot day after day, not knowing whither he went. Six months were spent in this wearisome travelling when, at the end of that period, he reached the capital of Sahasra Dal. He was passing by the palace-gate when the sighs and wailings of a woman sitting at the window of a house, on the road-side, attracted his attention. One moment's look, and they recognised each other. They continued to hold secret communications. Champa Dal heard everything, including the story of her vow, the period of which was to terminate the following day. It is customary, on the fulfilment of a vow, for some learned Brahman to make public recitations of events connected with the vow and the person who makes it. It was settled that Champa Dal should take upon himself the functions of the reciter. Accordingly, next morning, when it was proclaimed by beat of drum that the king wanted a learned Brahman who could recite the story of Keshavati on the fulfilment of her vow, Champa Dal touched the drum and said that he would make the recitation. Next morning a gorgeous assembly was held in the courtyard of the palace under a huge canopy of silk. The old king, Sahasra Dal, all the courtiers and the learned Brahmans of the country, were present there. Keshavati was also there behind a screen that she might not be exposed to the rude gaze of the people. Champa Dal, the reciter, sitting on a dais, began the story of Keshavati, as we have related it, from the beginning, commencing with the words—"There was a poor and half-witted Brahman, etc." As he was going on with the story, the reciter every now and then asked Keshavati behind the screen whether the story was correct; to which question she as often replied, "Quite correct; go on, Brahman." During the recitation of the story the Rakshasi maid-servant grew pale, as she perceived that her real character was discovered; and Sahasra Dal was astonished at the knowledge of the reciter regarding the history of his own life. The moment the story was finished, Sahasra Dal jumped up from his seat, and embracing the reciter, said, "You can be none other than my brother Champa Dal." Then the prince, inflamed with rage, ordered the maid-servant into his presence. A large hole, as deep as the height of a man, was dug in the ground; the maid-servant was put into it in a standing posture;

prickly thorn was heaped around her up to the crown of her head: in this wise was the maid-servant buried alive. After this Sahasra Dal and his princess, and Champa Dal and Keshavati, lived happily together many years.

1. Rakshasas and Rakshasis (male and female) are in Hindu mythology huge giants and giantesses, or rather demons. The word means literally raw-eaters; they were probably the chiefs of the aborigines whom the Aryans overthrew on their first settlement in the country.
2. Dasi is a general name for all maid-servants.
3. Sphatika is crystal, and sthambha pillar.
4. Bathing-place, either in a tank or on the bank of a river, generally furnished with flights of steps.

5

The Story of Swet-Basanta

There was a rich merchant who had an only son whom he loved passionately. He gave to his son whatever he wanted. His son wanted a beautiful house in the midst of a large garden. The house was built for him, and the grounds were laid out into a fine garden. One day as the merchant's son was walking in his garden, he put his hand into the nest of a small bird called toontooni, and found in it an egg, which he took and put in an almirah which was dug into the wall of his house. He closed the door of the almirah, and thought no more of the egg.

Though the merchant's son had a house of his own, he had no separate establishment; at any rate he kept no cook, for his mother used to send him regularly his breakfast and dinner every day. The egg which he deposited in the wall-almirah one day burst, and out of it came a beautiful infant, a girl. But the merchant's son knew nothing about it. He had forgotten everything about the egg, and the door of the wall-almirah had been kept closed, though not locked, ever since the day the egg was put there. The child grew up within the wall-almirah without the knowledge of the merchant's son or of any one else. When the child could walk, it had the curiosity one day to open the door; and seeing some food on the floor (the breakfast of the merchant's son sent by his mother), it came out, and ate a little of it, and returned to its cell in the wall-almirah. As the mother of the merchant's son sent him always more than he could himself eat, he perceived no diminution in the quantity. The girl of the wall-almirah used every day to come out and eat a part of the food, and after eating used to return to her place in the almirah. But as the girl got older and older, she began to eat more and more; hence the merchant's son began to perceive a diminution in the quantity of his food. Not dreaming of the existence of the wall-almirah girl, he wondered that his mother should send him such a small quantity of food. He sent word to his mother, complaining of the insufficiency of his meals, and of the slovenly manner in which the food was served up in the dish; for the girl of the wall-almirah used to finger the rice, curry, and other articles of food, and as she always went in a hurry back into the almirah that she might not be perceived by any one, she had no time to put the rice and the other things into proper order after she had eaten part of them. The mother was astonished at her son's complaint, for she gave always a much larger quantity than she knew her son could consume, and the food was served up on a silver plate neatly by her own hand. But as her son repeated the same complaint day after day, she began to suspect foul play. She told her son to watch and see whether any one ate part of it unperceived. Accordingly, one day when the servant brought the breakfast and laid it in a clean place on the floor, the merchant's son, instead of going to bathe as it had hitherto been his custom, hid himself in a secret place and began to watch. In a few minutes he saw the door of the wall-almirah open; a beautiful damsel of sweet sixteen stepped out of it, sat on the carpet spread before the breakfast, and began to eat. The merchant's son came out of his hiding-place, and the damsel could not escape. "Who are you, beautiful creature? You do not seem to be earth-born. Are you one of the daughters of the gods?" asked the merchant's son. The girl replied, "I do not know who I am. This I know, that one day I found myself in yonder almirah, and have been ever since living in it." The merchant's son thought it strange. He now remembered that sixteen years before he had put in the almirah an egg he had found in the nest of a toontooni bird. The uncommon beauty of the wall-almirah girl made a deep impression on the mind of the merchant's son, and he resolved in his mind to marry her. The girl no more went into the almirah, but lived in one of the rooms of the spacious house of the merchant's son.

The next day the merchant's son sent word to his mother to the effect that he would like to get married. His mother reproached herself for not having long before thought of her son's marriage, and sent a message to her son to the effect that she and his father would the next day send ghataks[1] to different countries to seek for a suitable bride. The merchant's son sent word that he had secured for himself a most lovable young lady, and that if his parents had no objections he would produce her before them. Accordingly the young lady of the wall-almirah was taken to the merchant's house; and the merchant and his wife were so struck with the matchless beauty, grace, and loveliness of the stranger, that, without asking any questions as to her birth, the nuptials were celebrated.

In course of time the merchant's son had two sons; the elder he named Swet and the younger Basanta. The old merchant died and so did his wife. Swet and Basanta grew up fine lads, and the elder was in due time married. Some time after Swet's marriage his mother, the wall-almirah lady, also died, and the widower lost no time in marrying a young and beautiful wife. As Swet's wife was older than his stepmother, she became the mistress of the house. The stepmother, like all stepmothers, hated Swet and Basanta with a perfect hatred; and the two ladies were naturally often at loggerheads with each other.

The Girl of the Wall-Almirah

It so happened one day that a fisherman brought to the merchant (we shall no longer call him the merchant's son, as his father had died) a fish of singular beauty. It was unlike any other fish that had been seen. The fish had marvellous qualities ascribed to it by the fisherman. If any one eats it, said he, when he laughs maniks[2] will drop from his mouth, and when he weeps pearls will drop from his eyes. The merchant, hearing of the wonderful properties of the fish, bought it at one thousand rupees, and put it into the hands of Swet's wife, who was the mistress of the house, strictly enjoining on her to cook it well and to give it to him alone to eat. The mistress, or house-mother, who had overheard the conversation between her father-in-law and the fisherman, secretly resolved in her mind to give the cooked fish to her husband and to his brother to eat, and to give to her father-in-law instead a frog daintily cooked. When she had finished cooking both the fish and the frog, she heard the noise of a squabble between her stepmother-in-law and her husband's brother. It appears that Basanta, who was but a lad yet, was passionately fond of pigeons, which he tamed. One of these pigeons had flown into the room of his stepmother, who had secreted it in her clothes. Basanta rushed into the room, and loudly demanded the pigeon. His stepmother denied any knowledge of the pigeon, on which the elder brother, Swet, forcibly took out the bird from her clothes and gave it to his brother. The stepmother cursed and swore, and added, "Wait, when the head of the house comes home I will make him shed the blood of you both before I give him water to drink." Swet's wife called her husband and said to him, "My dearest lord, that woman is a most wicked woman, and has boundless influence over my father-in-law. She will make him do what she has threatened. Our life is in imminent danger. Let us first eat a little, and let us all three run away from this place." Swet forthwith called Basanta to him, and told him what he had heard from his wife. They resolved to run away before nightfall. The woman placed before her husband and her brother-in-law the fish of wonderful properties, and they ate of it heartily. The woman packed up all her jewels in a box. As there was only one horse, and it was of uncommon fleetness, the three sat upon it; Swet held the reins, the woman sat in the middle with the jewel-box in her lap, and Basanta brought up the rear.

The horse galloped with the utmost swiftness. They passed through many a plain and many a noted town, till after midnight they found themselves in a forest not far from the bank of a river. Here the most untoward event took place. Swet's wife began to feel the pains of child-birth. They dismounted, and in an hour or two Swet's wife gave birth to a son. What were the two brothers to do in this forest? A fire must be kindled to give heat both to the mother and the new-born baby. But where was the fire to be got? There were no human habitations visible. Still fire must be procured—and it was the month of December— or else both the mother and the baby would certainly perish. Swet told Basanta to sit beside his wife, while he set out in the darkness of the night in search of fire.

Swet walked many a mile in darkness. Still he saw no human habitations. At last the genial light of Sukra[3] somewhat illumined his path, and he saw at a distance what seemed a large city.

"On a sudden an elephant gorgeously caparisoned shot across his path"

He was congratulating himself on his journey's end and on his being able to obtain fire for the benefit of his poor wife lying cold in the forest with the new-born babe, when on a sudden an elephant, gorgeously caparisoned, shot across his path, and gently taking him up by his trunk, placed him on the rich howdah[4] on its back. It then walked rapidly towards the city. Swet was quite taken aback. He did not understand the meaning of the elephant's action, and wondered what was in store for him. A crown was in store for him. In that kingdom, the chief city of which he was approaching, every morning a king was elected, for the king of the previous day was always found dead in the morning in the room of the queen. What caused the death of the king no one knew; neither did the queen herself (for every successive king took her to wife) know the cause. And the elephant who took hold of Swet was the king-maker. Early in the morning it went about, sometimes to distant places, and whosoever was brought on its back was acknowledged king by the people. The elephant majestically marched through the crowded streets of the city, amid the acclamations of the people, the meaning of which Swet did not understand, entered the palace, and placed him on the throne. He was proclaimed king amid the rejoicings of some and the lamentations of others. In the course of the day he heard of the strange fatality which overtook every night the elected king of those realms, but being possessed of great discretion and courage, he took every precaution to avert the dreadful catastrophe. Yet he hardly knew what expedients to adopt, as he was unacquainted with the nature of the danger. He resolved, however, upon two things, and these were, to go armed into the queen's bedchamber, and to sit up awake the whole night. The queen was young and of exquisite beauty, and so guileless and benevolent was the expression of her face that it was impossible from looking at her to suppose that she could use any foul means of taking away the life of her nightly consort. In the queen's chamber Swet spent a very agreeable evening; as the night advanced the queen fell asleep, but Swet kept awake, and was on the alert, looking at every creek and corner of the room, and expecting every minute to be murdered. In the dead of night he perceived something like a thread coming out of the left nostril of the queen. The thread was so thin that it was almost invisible. As he watched it he found it several yards long, and yet it was coming out. When the whole of it had come out, it began to grow thick, and in a few minutes it assumed the form of a huge serpent. In a moment Swet cut off the head of the serpent, the body of which wriggled violently. He sat quiet in the room, expecting other adventures. But nothing else happened. The queen slept longer than usual as she had been relieved of the huge snake which had made her stomach its den. Early next morning the ministers came expecting as usual to hear of the king's death; but when the ladies of the bedchamber knocked at the door of the queen they were astonished to see Swet come out. It was then known to all the people how that every night a terrible snake issued from the queen's nostrils, how it devoured the king every night, and how it had at last been killed by the fortunate Swet. The whole country rejoiced in the prospect of a permanent king. It is a strange thing, nevertheless it is true, that Swet did not remember his poor wife with the new-born babe lying in the forest, nor his brother attending on her. With the possession of the throne he seemed to forget the whole of his past history.

Basanta, to whom his brother had entrusted his wife and child, sat watching for many a weary hour, expecting every moment to see Swet return with fire. The whole night passed away without his return. At sunrise he went to the bank of the river which was close by, and anxiously looked about for his brother, but in vain. Distressed beyond measure, he sat on the river side and wept. A boat was passing by in which a merchant was returning to his country. As the boat was not far from the shore the merchant saw Basanta weeping; and what struck the attention of the merchant was the heap of what looked like pearls near the weeping man. At the request of the merchant the boatman took his vessel towards the bank; the merchant went to the weeping man, and found that the heap was a heap of real pearls of the finest lustre: and what astonished him most of all was that the heap was increasing every second, for the tear-drops that were falling from his eyes fell to the ground not as tears but as pearls. The merchant stowed away the heap of pearls into his boat, and with the help of his servants caught hold of Basanta himself, put him on board the vessel, and tied him to a post. Basanta, of course, resisted; but what could he do against so many? Thinking of his brother, his brother's wife and baby, and his own captivity, Basanta wept more bitterly than before, which mightily pleased the merchant, as the more tears his captive shed the richer he himself became. When the merchant reached his native town he confined Basanta in a room, and at stated hours every day scourged him in order to make him shed tears, every one of which was converted into a bright pearl. The merchant one day said to his servants, "As the fellow is making me rich by his weeping, let us see what he gives me by laughing." Accordingly he began to tickle his captive, on which Basanta laughed, and as he laughed a great many maniks dropped from his mouth. After this poor Basanta was alternately whipped and tickled all the day and far into the night; and the merchant, in consequence, became the wealthiest man in the land. Leaving Basanta subjected to the alternate processes of castigation and titillation, let us attend to the fortunes of the poor wife of Swet, alone in the forest, with a child just born.

Swet's wife, apparently deserted by her husband and her

brother-in-law, was overwhelmed with grief. A woman, but a few hours since delivered of a child—and her first child, alone, and in a forest, far from the habitations of men,—her case was indeed pitiable. She wept rivers of tears. Excessive grief, however, brought her relief. She fell asleep with the new-born baby in her arms. It so happened that at that hour the Kotwal (prefect of the police) of the country was passing that way. He had been very unfortunate with regard to his offspring; every child his wife presented him with died shortly after birth, and he was now going to bury the last infant on the banks of the river. As he was going, he saw in the forest a woman sleeping with a baby in her arms. It was a lively and beautiful boy. The Kotwal coveted the lovely infant. He quietly took it up, put in its place his own dead child, and returning home, told his wife that the child had not really died and had revived. Swet's wife, unconscious of the deceit practised upon her by the Kotwal, on waking found her child dead. The distress of her mind may be imagined. The whole world became dark to her. She was distracted with grief, and in her distraction she formed the resolution of committing suicide. The river was not far from the spot, and she determined to drown herself in it. She took in her hand the bundle of jewels and proceeded to the river-side. An old Brahman was at no great distance, performing his morning ablutions. He noticed the woman going into the water, and naturally thought that she was going to bathe; but when he saw her going far into deep waters, some suspicion arose in his mind. Discontinuing his devotions, he bawled out and ordered the woman to come to him. Swet's wife seeing that it was an old man that was calling her, retraced her steps and came to him. On being asked what she was about to do, she said that she was going to make an end of herself, and that as she had some jewels with her she would be obliged if he would accept them as a present. At the request of the old Brahman she related to him her whole story. The upshot was, that she was prevented from drowning herself, and that she was received into the Brahman's family, where she was treated by the Brahman's wife as her own daughter.

Years passed on. The reputed son of the Kotwal grew up a vigorous, robust lad. As the house of the old Brahman was not far from the Kotwal's, the Kotwal's son used accidentally to meet the handsome strange woman who passed for the Brahman's daughter. The lad liked the woman, and wanted to marry her. He spoke to his father about the woman, and the father spoke to the Brahman. The Brahman's rage knew no bounds. What! the infidel Kotwal's son aspiring to the hand of a Brahman's daughter! A dwarf may as well aspire to catch hold of the moon! But the Kotwal's son determined to have her by force. With this wicked object he one day scaled the wall that encompassed the Brahman's house, and got upon the thatched roof of the Brahman's cow-house. While he was reconnoitering from that lofty position, he heard the following conversation between two calves in the cow-house:—

First Calf. Men accuse us of brutish ignorance and immorality; but in my opinion men are fifty times worse.

Second Calf. What makes you say so, brother? Have you witnessed to-day any instance of human depravity?

First Calf. Who can be a greater monster of crime than the same lad who is at this moment standing on the thatched roof of this hut over our head?

Second Calf. Why, I thought it was only the son of our Kotwal; and I never heard that he was exceptionally vicious.

First Calf. You never heard, but now you hear from me. This wicked lad is now wishing to get married to his own mother!

The First Calf then related to the inquisitive Second Calf in full the story of Swet and Basanta; how they and Swet's wife fled from the vengeance of their stepmother; how Swet's wife was delivered of a child in the forest by the river-side; how Swet was made king by the elephant, and how he succeeded in killing the serpent which issued out of the queen's nostrils; how Basanta was carried away by the merchant, confined in a dungeon, and alternately flogged and tickled for pearls and maniks; how the Kotwal exchanged his dead child for the living one of Swet; how Swet's wife was prevented from drowning herself in the river by the Brahman; how she was received into the Brahman's family and treated as his daughter; how the Kotwal's son grew up a hardy, lusty youth, and fell in love with her; and how at that very moment he was intent on accomplishing his brutal object. All this story the Kotwal's son heard from the thatched roof of the cow-house, and was struck with horror. He forthwith got down from the thatch, and went home and told his father that he must have an interview with the king. Notwithstanding his reputed father's protestations to the contrary, he had an interview with the king, to whom he repeated the whole story as he had overheard it from the thatch of the cow-house. The king now remembered his poor wife's case. She was brought from the house of the Brahman, whom he richly rewarded, and put her in her proper position as the queen of the kingdom; the reputed son of the Kotwal was acknowledged as his own son, and proclaimed the heir-apparent to the throne; Basanta was brought out of the dungeon, and the wicked merchant who had maltreated him was buried alive in the earth surrounded with thorns. After this, Swet, his wife and son, and Basanta, lived together happily for many years.

1. Professional match-makers.
2. Manik, or rather manikya, is a fabulous precious stone of incredible value. It is found on the head of some species of snakes, and is equal in value to the wealth of seven kings.
3. Venus, the Morning Star.
4. The seat on the back of an elephant.

6

The Evil Eye of Sani

Once upon a time Sani, or Saturn, the god of bad luck, and Lakshmi, the goddess of good luck, fell out with each other in heaven. Sani said he was higher in rank than Lakshmi, and Lakshmi said she was higher in rank than Sani. As all the gods and goddesses of heaven were equally ranged on either side, the contending deities agreed to refer the matter to some human being who had a name for wisdom and justice. Now, there lived at that time upon earth a man of the name of Sribatsa,[1] who was as wise and just as he was rich. Him, therefore, both the god and the goddess chose as the settler of their dispute. One day, accordingly, Sribatsa was told that Sani and Lakshmi were wishing to pay him a visit to get their dispute settled. Sribatsa was in a fix. If he said Sani was higher in rank than Lakshmi, she would be angry with him and forsake him. If he said Lakshmi was higher in rank than Sani, Sani would cast his evil eye upon him. Hence he made up his mind not to say anything directly, but to leave the god and the goddess to gather his opinion from his action. He got two stools made, the one of gold and the other of silver, and placed them beside him. When Sani and Lakshmi came to Sribatsa, he told Sani to sit upon the silver stool, and Lakshmi upon the gold stool. Sani became mad with rage, and said in an angry tone to Sribatsa, "Well, as you consider me lower in rank than

Lakshmi, I will cast my eye on you for three years; and I should like to see how you fare at the end of that period." The god then went away in high dudgeon. Lakshmi, before going away, said to Sribatsa, "My child, do not fear. I'll befriend you." The god and the goddess then went away.

Sribatsa said to his wife, whose name was Chintamani, "Dearest, as the evil eye of Sani will be upon me at once, I had better go away from the house; for if I remain in the house with you, evil will befall you and me; but if I go away, it will overtake me only." Chintamani said, "That cannot be; wherever you go, I will go, your lot shall be my lot." The husband tried hard to persuade his wife to remain at home; but it was of no use. She would go with her husband. Sribatsa accordingly told his wife to make an opening in their mattress, and to stow away in it all the money and jewels they had. On the eve of leaving their house, Sribatsa invoked Lakshmi, who forthwith appeared. He then said to her, "Mother Lakshmi! as the evil eye of Sani is upon us, we are going away into exile; but do thou befriend us, and take care of our house and property." The goddess of good luck answered, "Do not fear; I'll befriend you; all will be right at last." They then set out on their journey. Sribatsa rolled up the mattress and put it on his head. They had not gone many miles when they saw a river before them. It was not fordable; but there was a canoe there with a man sitting in it. The travellers requested the ferryman to take them across. The ferryman said, "I can take only one at a time; but you are three—yourself, your wife, and the mattress." Sribatsa proposed that first his wife and the mattress should be taken across, and then he; but the ferryman would not hear of it. "Only one at a time," repeated he; "first let me take across the mattress." When the canoe with the mattress was in the middle of the stream, a fierce gale arose, and carried away the mattress, the canoe, and the ferryman, no one knows whither. And it was strange the stream also disappeared, for the place, where they saw a few minutes since the rush of waters, had now become firm ground. Sribatsa then knew that this was nothing but the evil eye of Sani.

Sribatsa and his wife, without a pice in their pocket, went to a village which was hard by. It was dwelt in for the most part by wood-cutters, who used to go at sunrise to the forest to cut wood, which they sold in a town not far from the village. Sribatsa proposed to the wood-cutters that he should go along with them to cut wood.

"They then set out on their journey"

They agreed. So he began to fell trees as well as the best of them; but there was this difference between Sribatsa and the other wood-cutters, that whereas the latter cut any and every sort of wood, the former cut only precious wood like sandal-wood. The wood-cutters used to bring to market large loads of common wood, and Sribatsa only a few pieces of sandal-wood, for which he got a great deal more money than the others. As this was going on day after day, the wood-cutters through envy plotted together, and drove away from the village Sribatsa and his wife.

The next place they went to was a village of weavers, or rather cotton-spinners. Here Chintamani, the wife of Sribatsa, made herself useful by spinning cotton. And as she was an intelligent and skilful woman, she spun finer thread than the other women; and she got more money. This roused the envy of the native women of the village. But this was not all. Sribatsa, in order to gain the good grace of the weavers, asked them to a feast, the dishes of which were all cooked by his wife. As Chintamani excelled in cooking, the barbarous weavers of the village were quite charmed by the delicacies set before them. When the men went to their homes, they reproached their wives for not being able to cook so well as the wife of Sribatsa, and called them good-for-nothing women. This thing made the women of the village hate Chintamani the more. One day Chintamani went to the river-side to bathe along with the other women of the village. A boat had been lying on the bank stranded on the sand for many days; they had tried to move it, but in vain. It so happened that as Chintamani by accident touched the boat, it moved off to the river. The boatmen, astonished at the event, thought that the woman had uncommon power, and might be useful on similar occasions in future. They therefore caught hold of her, put her in the boat, and rowed off. The women of the village, who were present, did not offer any resistance as they hated Chintamani. When Sribatsa heard how his wife had been carried away by boatmen, he became mad with grief. He left the village, went to the river-side, and resolved to follow the course of the stream till he should meet the boat where his wife was a prisoner. He travelled on and on, along the side of the river, till it became dark. As there were no huts to be seen, he climbed into a tree for the night. Next morning as he got down from the tree he saw at the foot of it a cow called a Kapila-cow, which never calves, but which gives milk at all hours of the day whenever it is milked. Sribatsa milked the cow, and drank its milk to his heart's content. He was astonished to find that the cow-dung which lay on the ground was of a bright yellow colour; indeed, he found it was pure gold. While it was in a soft state he wrote his own name upon it, and when in the course of the day it became hardened, it looked like a brick of gold—and so it was. As the tree grew on the river-side, and as the Kapila-cow came morning and evening to supply him with milk, Sribatsa resolved to stay there till he should meet the boat. In the meantime the gold-bricks were increasing in number every day, for the cow both morning and evening deposited there the precious article. He put the gold-bricks, upon all of which his name was engraved, one upon another in rows, so that from a distance they looked like a hillock of gold.

Leaving Sribatsa to arrange his gold-bricks under the tree on the river-side we must follow the fortunes of his wife. Chintamani was a woman of great beauty; and thinking that her beauty might be her ruin, she, when seized by the boatmen, offered to Lakshmi the following prayer——"O Mother Lakshmi! have pity upon me. Thou hast made me beautiful, but now my beauty will undoubtedly prove my ruin by the loss of honour and chastity. I therefore beseech thee, gracious Mother, to make me ugly, and to cover my body with some loathsome disease, that the boatmen may not touch me." Lakshmi heard Chintamani's prayer; and in the twinkling of an eye, while she was in the arms of the boatmen, her naturally beautiful form was turned into a vile carcase. The boatmen, on putting her down in the boat, found her body covered with loathsome sores which were giving out a disgusting stench. They therefore threw her into the hold of the boat amongst the cargo, where they used morning and evening to send her a little boiled rice and some water. In that hold Chintamani had a miserable life of it; but she greatly preferred that misery to the loss of chastity. The boatmen went to some port, sold the cargo, and were returning to their country when the sight of what seemed a hillock of gold, not far from the river-side, attracted their attention. Sribatsa, whose eyes were ever directed towards the river, was delighted when he saw a boat turn towards the bank, as he fondly imagined his wife might be in it. The boatmen went to the hillock of gold, when Sribatsa said that the gold was his. They put all the gold-bricks on board their vessel, took Sribatsa prisoner, and put him into the hold not far from the woman covered with sores. They of course immediately recognised each other, in spite of the change Chintamani had undergone, but thought it prudent not to speak to each other. They communicated their ideas, therefore, by signs and gestures. Now, the boatmen were fond of playing at dice, and as Sribatsa appeared to them from his looks to be a respectable man, they always asked him to join in the game. As he was an expert player, he almost always won the game, on which the boatmen, envying his superior skill, threw him overboard. Chintamani had the presence of mind, at that moment, to throw into the water a pillow which she had for resting her head upon. Sribatsa took hold of the pillow, by means of which he floated down the stream till he was carried at nightfall to what seemed a garden on the water's edge. There he stuck among the trees, where he remained the whole night, wet and shivering. Now, the garden belonged to an old widow who was in former years the chief flower-supplier to the king of that country. Through some cause or other a blight seemed to have come over her garden, as almost all the trees and plants ceased flowering; she had therefore given up her place as the flower-supplier of the royal household. On the morning following the night on which Sribatsa had stuck among the trees, however, the old woman on getting up from her bed could scarcely believe her eyes when she saw the whole garden ablaze with flowers. There was not a single tree or plant which was not begemmed with flowers. Not understanding the cause of such a miraculous sight, she took a walk through the garden, and found on the river's brink, stuck among the trees, a man shivering and almost dying with cold. She brought him to her cottage, lighted a fire to give him warmth, and showed him every attention, as she ascribed the wonderful flowering of her trees to his presence. After making him as comfortable as she could, she ran to the king's palace, and told his chief servants that she was again in a position to supply the palace with flowers; so she was restored to her former office as the flower-woman of the royal household. Sribatsa, who stopped a few days with the woman, requested her to recommend him to one of the king's ministers for a berth. He was accordingly sent for to the palace, and as he was at once found to be a man of intelligence, the king's minister asked him what post he would like to have. Agreeably to his wish he was appointed collector of tolls on the river. While discharging his duties as river toll-gatherer, in the course of a few days he saw the very boat in which his wife was a prisoner. He detained the boat, and charged the boatmen with the theft of gold-bricks which he claimed as his own. At the mention of gold-bricks the king himself came to the river-side, and was astonished beyond measure to see bricks made of gold, every one of which had the inscription—Sribatsa. At the same time Sribatsa rescued from the boatmen his wife, who, the moment she came out of the vessel, became as lovely as before. The king heard the story of Sribatsa's misfortunes from his lips, entertained him in a princely style for many days, and at last sent him and his wife to their own country with presents of horses and elephants. The evil eye of Sani was now turned away from Sribatsa, and he again became what he formerly was, the Child of Fortune.

1. Sri is another name of Lakshmi, and batsa means child; so that Sribatsa is
   literally the "child of fortune."